MONKEY PALACE

MONKEY PALACE

BILL LIGHTLE

Bill Lightle

ISBN-13: 978-1976560354
ISBN-10: 1976560357

Published by Bill Lightle
285 Kari Glen Drive
Fayetteville, GA 30215

This is a work of fiction.

This book is dedicated to David and Dylan.
Both heard my stories first.

And though you [America] have everything,
you are lacking one thing: God
—Nicaraguan poet, Rubén Darío (1867-1916)

CHAPTER 1

JULY 1985

Inside the white station wagon with brown wooden panels, nylon rope bound the hands and feet of the two girls. Gray tape covered their mouths. Dark hoods covered their heads. The exchange was made a few minutes before midnight along a dirt road near a timber plantation south of Albany, Georgia. It only took three minutes.

Waiting for the station wagon was a windowless green Chevy van. There were two men inside. They got out of the van and stood in the middle of the road.

After the station wagon stopped, the driver and his partner walked to where the others were waiting.

"I have your order and they're in excellent shape," the driver of the station wagon said.

"Bring 'em out so we can see 'em," a man from the van said.

The girls were led from the station wagon to the men who had come for them. They were bound together by a rope and were led as if they were livestock on a plantation. Their hoods were removed.

"See, ain't they purty?" the driver of the station wagon said. "Ain't a scratch on 'em. They just wanna have a little fun. All yours now. Just one thing missin'."

"It's all there," the van's driver said. "You count it, we'll wait." He passed a black briefcase to the men who had brought the girls. The men from the station wagon counted the money while shining a flashlight into the briefcase.

"It's all there, just like we said," the other man from the van said.

When the counting ended and the briefcase was closed, the girls were loaded into the back of the van. Nothing else was said by the four men as they got into their vehicles and drove away in opposite directions.

*

Twenty minutes later, after the two kidnapped girls had been dropped off along the Kinchafoonee Creek just outside of Albany, the van arrived at the Monkey Palace, where the Friday night crowd was partying into Saturday morning. The Palace was one of the most popular nightclubs in Albany and included six adult rhesus monkeys in a large glass cage. The brown animals had orange-tinted rumps and legs, and often swung on the wooden poles and ropes inside the cage as people got drunk and danced to Earth, Wind & Fire. The monkeys were a spectacle, and people came not only to drink, dance, and find one-night love, but to see them.

The two men parked the van behind the Monkey Palace, went inside, and ordered drinks at the bar.

The Monkey Palace was not a large nightclub, and most nights it was packed. Wall-to-wall it could handle about a hundred people, but things would be tight. There was a dance floor near the monkeys, tables and chairs in the back, and a bar with ten red-cushioned stools. Strobe lights and dance music were constant from ten to two every night except Sunday, when it was closed.

From the tables in the back of the club, marijuana smoke sometimes filtered to the ceiling along with that of Marlboros. It was dark in the back of the Palace and rule breaking there was expected.

The general progression of those who reveled in Albany's nightlife began at Jim's Oyster Bar with a few beers in frosted mugs. Then cross the Flint River into east Albany for a couple of drinks at the Sand Trap, another nightclub with a dance floor. Then back across the river to the Monkey Palace.

By midnight at the Palace, and sometimes before, a line of people waiting to get in formed outside. A city ordinance required bars to close at two in the morning. But when the music was turned off and the lights were turned on at the Palace, the place was still packed. The owner often allowed patrons to stay sometimes until three or later. The dark eyes of the monkeys in the glass cage seemed confused by the behavior of their drunken cousins.

*

The two men from the green van sat at the bar in the Monkey Palace, sipping Jack Daniels over ice as the disc jockey played an album called *Silk Degrees* by Boz Scaggs. The dance floor was packed with about twenty couples slow dancing. For some it was not so much dancing after a night of drinking, but just hanging on to their partner.

The two men drank slowly and stirred their liquor with thin white plastic straws after each sip. They said nothing to each other or to anyone else until the bartender, called Sugar Baby, spoke.

"You two havin' a good night?"

"Yep, so far, Sugar Baby, bin one of the best," one of the men said.

"Yeah, that's right. One of the best nights ever," the second man said.

"Yeah, I know you two take good care of your business," Sugar Baby said. "I know that's right."

"We try to do our best," the first man said. "We always try."

Sugar Baby waited on other customers as the music and strobe lights and cigarette smoke filled the Palace. Then the two men finished their drinks, got up from the barstools, and walked through the crowded bar, out the back door to their van, and drove back to the Kinchafoonee Creek.

CHAPTER 2

My editor at the *Albany Chronicle*, Mickey Burke, called me to his desk a little before ten on a Monday morning. I had just finished writing a story about an armed robbery that happened around midnight downtown along Oglethorpe Boulevard. I had gotten my information earlier in the morning from the Albany Police Department on Pine Avenue across the street from the newsroom.

No one hurt, no one arrested. The man who reported the crime said the gunman took twelve dollars from him and a quart of unopened Schlitz Malt Liquor. I put that in my lede.

"Maynard, what do you got going now?" Mickey said.

Fifteen minutes earlier I'd handed him the copy of my armed robbery story typed on two pieces of tan paper connected by scotch tape. He had already edited it for tomorrow's edition. The *Chronicle* was a daily morning paper covering southwest Georgia, with about forty thousand subscribers in and around Albany.

I'd started working for the paper a few years earlier, in 1980, after graduating from Georgia Southwestern College in nearby Americus with a degree in political science. I loved the job.

"Nothing right now, Mickey. Nothing so far."

"Good, I got something for you."

"All right. What is it?"

Mickey told me he had just received a tip from one of his sources inside the Albany Police Department about a body that had been found near the Ramada Inn off Palmyra Road. The police were on the scene. I knew the area well. It was a five-minute drive north from the newsroom.

"Take your camera and go get what you can," Mickey said. "My source tells me it looks to be a woman. Maybe a teenager. Both our photographers are on assignments. Don't forget your camera."

"I got it, Mickey. I'm on my way."

"Whatever you get, we'll run it tomorrow."

"Okay. I'll see you when I get back."

I returned to my desk and took the black Nikon camera from the bottom drawer, and picked up a reporter's notepad and two black pens from the top of the desk. Some reporters in the newsroom were typing stories, while others were reading the morning paper.

I walked outside and got into my four-door brown Buick, pushed in a Bob Dylan eight-track tape, *Desire*, and drove north to where the body had been found. "Oh Sister" was the name of the song: *We grew up together/From the cradle to the grave/We died and were reborn/And then mysteriously saved.*

The skies were blue and the day had begun warm. It would be hot soon and stay hot for the next few months. A South Georgia summer had no mercy.

I drove north on Washington Street away from downtown Albany, turned onto Palmyra Road, passing the hospital with the same name and then passing the Monkey Palace, which would open at five that afternoon.

Last week I had taken Abby Sinclair there for drinks after work. This morning she had left the newsroom about nine to interview the newly-appointed executive director of the Albany Chamber of Commerce. When I played Dylan, I thought of her. Hell, almost no matter what I did, I thought of her.

I drove across Slappey Boulevard and passed the P2, another night-club where we sometimes went for after-work drinks, and the Ramada Inn, both on my right. I was getting close.

After passing the motel, I could see three marked Albany Police Department cars, an ambulance, and two dark blue Ford LTDs all parked on the right side of the road. The lawmen stood in an area of tall pines and underbrush about seventy-five yards from the road. Yellow tape had been strung across three pine trees, indicating an investigation was underway.

I counted ten lawmen, some in uniform and a few detectives in street clothes. Two emergency medical technicians stood near the body, which was covered with a white sheet. The EMTs had a gurney to transport the body.

I parked behind the police vehicles and walked toward the crime scene. As I got closer, one of the plain-clothes officers saw me. I knew a few on the force from earlier stories I had covered, but I didn't recognize the one walking toward me.

"That's far enough," he said. "This area's off limits. It's a crime scene and under investigation. Hold where you are."

I walked within thirty feet from the body and the men standing over it. Some of the lawmen walked slowly throughout the crime scene with their heads down looking for clues of the crime in the underbrush. I stopped walking and identified myself.

"Okay, I understand," I said, "but can you tell me what you know so far about the body?"

"Nope," the man said. "That ain't my job. Stay here and I'll see what I can do. See if I can find someone who can talk."

The officer left and I used a zoom lens to take several pictures of what was happening within those pine trees. I got a few clean shots of the sheet-covered body. I did it all in about thirty seconds. Then another detective approached me.

"Who are you with?" he said.

"I'm John Maynard with the *Chronicle*. We got a call this morning about the body. My editor, Mickey Burke, sent me out."

"I know who you are, Maynard. I don't think we've ever met, but I read what you write. You get it right most of the time."

"Thanks. What can you tell me about what's happening here?"

"Okay, Maynard, since you're out here, I'll give you what I got. I'm Detective Vince McGill. Here's what we have."

McGill had gray hair and was around six feet tall. He wore a tan suit but not a tie. This was the first time I had met him during my time with the paper. I'd seen him at press briefings and knew he had been on the force for many years. He had a reputation for thoroughness that some of his peers lacked. He seemed to be in charge of the investigation, I thought.

I had my camera strapped around my neck, and I took a pen and notepad out of my back pocket. Detective McGill began to talk and I wrote. He was concise with his words and spoke in a slow manner, allowing me to take good notes that weren't rushed.

The words he spoke horrified me.

McGill told me they had found the body of a naked a teenager, around fifteen or sixteen. She had dark eyes and long dark hair. Her arms and legs had been broken, other bones too. Her skull was fractured. Her body had been cut many times by what appeared to be a thin, sharp knife.

He didn't say it this way, but the girl had been tortured.

When she was alive, she had been a beautiful young girl. The evil things done to her had made her ugly in death. Her hands and feet had been bound with thick white nylon rope. She wore a slender chain and silver crucifix around her neck. McGill stopped his story, took a deep breath, and looked toward Palmyra Road where cop cars were parked. It was a long pause between us.

"Maynard?"

"What is it, Detective McGill?"

"This is my twenty-eighth year being a cop. The last fifteen I've been a detective. I've seen a lot. Nothing like this."

"I'm sorry you had to see this awful thing."

"Me too. It was too much for one of my boys. Young detective who has a ten year old girl. He saw the victim and ran off into the trees and lost his eggs and bacon. *Jesus,* somebody tortured that poor girl. What must've been going through her mind when it was happening to her? I can't imagine. No one can."

I waited a few moments before speaking. Both of us looked at the body and the men combing the area in search of evidence to this crime.

"Detective, I know you just found her, but do you have any leads on who did this to her?"

"I wish I could tell you we do. But we have nothing at this point. She was found naked, and like I said, no ID. We'll be here awhile today. Our investigation is underway. I can promise you this, we'll find who did this. I promise you that."

"No idea who she is?"

"Nope. I've said more than once now. We don't know. I wish we did know. God, but I'd hate to explain this to the girl's family."

"Can you tell me who found her?"

"We got a call this morning from a woman who lives in the neighborhood. Said her son was bike riding through these trees and saw the girl. Schools are out for the summer. Lots of kids around here. Helluva a thing for a boy to see. For anybody to see."

"When did the call come in?"

"About an hour ago. We were here five minutes later. Y'all must have a good source in the department."

"We do all right."

I continued taking notes while the lawmen investigating the scene extended their search in the underbrush. They moved slow, heads down as their feet swept through the tall grass.

"Have you had a chance to talk to anyone in the neighborhood?"

"Not yet, but we'll get to them."

"Any idea how long she'd been lying there?"

"I'd say six to eight hours, but we won't know for sure until the coroner examines her later today."

"Do you think she was killed here, or somewhere else and brought here?"

"Can't say either way at this point. We just don't know. Too early."

"So she could've been killed elsewhere?"

"It's possible."

"When do you think you'll have an ID on her?" I said.

"I hope soon. We'll contact the GBI and FBI to determine if she matches any reports of missing persons. We'll contact local law enforcement agencies in our area. We'll see what turns up."

"About how old did you say she was?"

"My guess is fifteen or sixteen. It's a guess. A good guess."

"Anything else I need to know?" I said.

"No, that's about it."

"Thanks, Detective McGill. I'm sure I'll be following up on this."

"You know where to find me."

We shook hands, and the detective walked to where the body was still on the ground. He spoke to the EMTs who lifted the body onto a silver gurney. The white sheet was wrapped tight around her. The two men pushed the gurney past me, placed her into the ambulance, and drove away. I snapped a few more pictures of her before the body was loaded into the ambulance. Then I wrote additional notes describing the landscape where she had been found.

Not far from that spot was a baseball field I'd played on about ten years earlier, when I was growing up in Albany. I was just fifteen then.

CHAPTER 3

Before I returned to the newsroom, I drove down Ken Gardens Road to the Pony League Baseball field I played on when I was young. The field was just a few blocks from where she had been found. I was a teenager when I played baseball there. That was as long as the Palmyra Girl was allowed to live.

That's the name I would call her until I learned her actual name. Palmyra Girl found off Palmyra Road.

I pulled into the brown-dirt parking lot at the ball field, stopped, but didn't get out of my car. *Desire* was still playing. A group of boys, probably thirteen or fourteen years old, were playing ball. Two girls about the same age watched the boys play from the gray-wooden bleachers along the first base line. They both wore white shorts, had dark hair. Could've been sisters.

I played games at night on the same field when I was a teenager, and on Sundays after my family attended mass, my father would bring me here to hit ground balls. He hit them by the hundreds, and I became pretty good at fielding them. Those were good days. She was just fifteen.

I watched the boys hit fly balls and grounders to one another, some showing off for the two girls watching. The sun was rising higher. Summer days and summer fun. I watched them play for a few minutes and looked at the girls on the bleachers a final time before returning to the newsroom. Thoughts of death overcame thoughts of baseball.

Back at the office, I told Mickey the story and gave him my roll of film. I had shot about twenty pictures at the crime scene and he sent the film upstairs for development. He would edit my story and select the art that afternoon.

"No ID on the girl?" Mickey said.

"Not yet."

"What about an autopsy?"

"Detective McGill said he'll try to get one done soon. Probably today."

"Follow up this afternoon before you leave. We'll run it tomorrow. And follow up after that. See where it takes you. Got it?"

"Okay, Mickey. I got it."

Abby was still out of the newsroom working on a feature story about the Chamber's new director. I needed to talk to her. I needed to see her.

I sat at my desk and put a piece of tan typing paper in my black manual Royal typewriter. The writing was difficult. The story was not complicated. But the writing of it did not come easy to me like many other crime stories during the past few years. My gut told me why. So did my heart.

I often wrote about death. Murder, car crashes, the deaths of public officials. All part of my job. The kind of death the Palmyra Girl had suffered was something I had not written about. Words on paper were a struggle.

I worked more than an hour on the five-hundred word story. If I had been writing on a deadline, Mickey would've been justifiably raising hell. "Goddamn it Maynard, I need your story!" That's what he would've said.

He said it that way to me many times my first year in the news-room. He was never the sensitive kind. A smart man and a good editor, but he didn't give a shit about your feelings. Once I figured that out, things went well.

I was almost finished with my story when I got up from my desk to get a cup of coffee. I looked for Abby at her desk but she was still out. Fifteen minutes later, I had completed the story and saw Abby enter the newsroom with a white paper bag. I followed her to her desk and sat down in the black vinyl chair in front of her desk.

"Johnny Boy, I was thinking of you and brought you lunch."

"I been missing you."

"Well, here I am. Same as I always was."

"Good. That's what I needed to hear."

"Something wrong?"

"Nothing we can fix."

From her bag she pulled two ham and cheese sandwiches on toasted wheat bread she had bought from the Cookie Shop, a downtown eatery. She had one bag of barbeque chips and two cans of Coke. She put the food and drinks on her desk with a stack of napkins.

"Tell me your morning was better than mine, John. Imagine spending it at the chamber where everyone talks like a paid advertisement. How many more fake smiles can I endure?"

"So not much fun with the next executive director?"'

"You can read all about it Sunday in the Business Section. I'm sure you'll be transformed. And your morning?"

I told Abby everything I saw and heard that morning off Palmyra Road where the young boy had found the young girl's tortured body. The whole time I kept thinking of Detective McGill's description of her, "long black hair and dark eyes. She was a beautiful kid before this happened to her," he said.

I was in love with Abby, the girl with dark eyes and dark hair.

We started working for the paper about the same time. She was a couple years younger than me, having graduated from Valdosta State College with a journalism degree before joining the *Chronicle*. The first day I saw her, I was attracted to her.

Then I came to know how she thought, how she saw her place in the world, and her search for truth in all things. It was over for me.

She started on her sandwich as I began my story. As I continued talking, her eating stopped. I left out no detail McGill had given to me.

"Oh, John, there is evil in this world. It's awful to say it. Worse still to see it."

"Right here in our hometown. Don't have to go anywhere to find it, Abby."

"Poor girl. Just a teenager. Age doesn't matter, though. What must it have felt like? The fear and pain she went through, John. That poor girl."

"I can't get her out of my head. I didn't see her. I didn't ask to see her. If they had asked me, I would've said no. But I see her now in my head. She's stuck there."

"You didn't see the body, right?"

"No, I didn't. I do now."

"It'd be worse if you had seen her. It would have to be worse."

"It's bad now. But I have my life and she doesn't have hers."

"Is it your story now?" Abby said.

"Yeah, Mickey said so. I hope they arrest, convict, and send somebody to die in prison for what they did to her. Soon. Real soon."

"No ID yet?"

"No."

"What do you know about McGill?" Abby said.

"From everything I've heard, he's one of the better ones at the APD. Got a good reputation for smarts. Can't say that about some others I've met over there."

"I hope he knows what he's doing and doesn't give up easy."

"Me too."

"Her family, John. What about her family? What do you think they're going through?"

"Abby, the cops don't know who she is, and they don't know anything about her family. I told you that remember?"

"I know, I know. But how would you like to be the one to inform the family about her? Her suffering is over. Poor girl. Not her family's suffering. That hasn't begun yet."

"No, I don't want to be that person. I didn't even want to write the story."

I had not started the sandwich Abby had given me and decided to save it altogether. I had no appetite. She had taken a couple of bites from hers, but as my story unfolded she didn't return to her eating. Now she had no appetite. We had not opened the Cokes or the bag of chips.

"Mickey wants the story later this afternoon," I said. "I'm going to call McGill later to see if he can add to what I know. A case like this, they may've gone ahead with an autopsy. There may be some things I add to the story later this afternoon."

"You take care of it, John, and I'm going to write this piece for the Sunday paper. Our new leader of the Chamber of Commerce. Let's have a drink after work."

"Sounds good. I'll need one."

"I worry about you, John. You know I do."

"I need a little of your worry. Not too much, though. You should worry more about someone else."

"What do you mean?"

"I'm not the one whose life was ended before it ever got started. I'm not her mother, father, sister or brother. I don't even know them but I worry for them."

"I know, I know, I know. But I still worry about you, John."

Abby got up from the brown vinyl chair behind her desk and walked to me as I stood up to leave. She hugged me full with both arms wrapped around my back as she pressed her cheek against mine. Mickey looked at us as did two other reporters. I needed the hug and didn't know how much until I got it. I didn't give a shit who was watching.

A few hours later the telephone rang at my desk.

"John Maynard, *Albany Chronicle.*"

"This is McGill with the APD. You got a minute?"

"Yes, sir, I do. What do you have?"

"I got the autopsy report from the coroner. Just picked it up a few minutes ago. I wanted you to know what we have."

"Okay, thanks. Let's hear it."

The Palmyra Girl had a total of thirty-three broken bones. The cause of death was likely a blow to her skull with a heavy, solid object. She lost almost one-third of her blood supply from twenty separate cuts on her body. She probably died six to eight hours before the neighborhood boy spotted her under the pine trees and in the tall grass.

She appeared to be of Hispanic descent. She was a small girl, only about five feet four and a hundred and five pounds. I took notes the whole time he spoke.

"Had she been raped before her death?"

"Same question I asked. The coroner said it appeared so."

"Anything else I need to know from the coroner's report?"

"Well, I got a copy of it and you're welcome to walk over and see it."

"I'm on my way."

I told Mickey where I was headed and crossed Pine Avenue and found Detective McGill in his office on the bottom floor of the courthouse. Unlike most other detectives, he didn't smoke. He offered me a cup of coffee and I accepted. I sat down in a brown metal chair with a green seat cushion in front of his desk. His desk was uncluttered. A telephone, an electric typewriter, and stack of brown folders. All seemed to fit like pieces in a puzzle.

He handed me the coroner's report, and I read it twice. It only took me a couple of minutes. I didn't take any notes from it and returned it to McGill. There was nothing for me to add to my story. McGill had been thorough with what he had told me over the telephone.

"Looks like you covered it pretty well," I said. "Any additional information on your investigation? Any idea where she was killed? Do you have any ID on her yet?"

"The answer is still no to all those questions. We'll find out who she is, and we'll find out who did this to her. I promise you that."

"Detective, I got a question for you."

"I'm not surprised. What is it?"

"How many Hispanic families live in and around Albany? Any idea?"

"No good numbers. Can't be many. We get some in the area that come through, work on the farms, and move on when the picking is done."

"That's about what I thought."

Detective McGill opened the front drawer of his gray metal desk and removed something. It was small and he held it in the palm of his right hand. I couldn't see what he had.

"I wanted to show you this. I mentioned it to you this morning."

He opened his hand and there was a silver crucifix attached to a silver chain. Both the crucifix and chain were shiny and looked new.

"This is what she was wearing?" I said.

"It was around her neck when we found her. So far, other than her body, it's our only piece of evidence."

He handed the crucifix to me.

"This morning there wasn't enough light under those trees for me to read what's inscribed on the crucifix. After I got back to the office, I was able to clearly read it. Take a look. Can you read it?"

I looked at the chain and crucifix and read what was on it. It was in English.

"I see the word MARIA in capital letters," I said. "And it says, GOD IS LOVE."

CHAPTER 4

After I updated my story with the information from the coroner's report, I gave the copy to Mickey for editing, then I left the newsroom with Abby. It was a few minutes before five.

She was driving her blue Plymouth Duster that she referred to as Baby Blue, in appreciation of a Bob Dylan song. She sometimes talked to her car like a mother does to a newborn, with love and care.

I followed her in my four-door brown Buick for which I had no affectionate terms. We were headed to the Monkey Palace for drinks. I needed one. Maybe more.

Bob "Big Foot" DuBose owned the Monkey Palace. He was in his late thirties and lived on Lover's Lane Road, just outside of Albany on Lake Chehaw. The lake was named after a Creek Indian village in the area before the 1830s, when whites moved in and one culture replaced another.

Bob was almost six four and weighed about a hundred and seventy pounds. Sometimes his friends called him Bean Pole Bob or Flag Pole. Mostly they called him Big Foot. He wore a size fourteen, some said fifteen, black high-top Chuck Taylor Converse tennis shoes, or he went barefooted. If he wasn't working at the Palace, he was barefooted. Bob's feet were big enough to water ski without a ski. He was damn good at it, too.

Bob had dropped out of high school in the late sixties, spent a few years in the Navy during the Vietnam War, returned to Albany, worked in construction building homes, and bartended at night before borrowing money from an uncle to open the Palace. Neither one of them thought the place would make any money. They were both wrong.

It was Bob's idea about the monkeys, and his uncle gave him hell about it. "Damn, son, ain't nobody gonna wanna see damn monkeys when they drinkin' and tryin' to get some cooter," his uncle said. Bob got the money anyway.

Big Foot said the idea about the monkeys came to him one night after drinking a half case of Budweiser, smoking three joints, and watching an episode of *Mutual of Omaha's Wild Kingdom* about monkeys. That's the story Bob told if you asked him, and it didn't matter to him whether you believed him or not.

"I saw those monkeys lookin' at me from the TV and I knew then what to do," Bob said. "It was like they were tellin' me what to do." He would never attribute any of this to the beer and the pot.

Bob had been married and divorced twice during the six years he had owned the Monkey Palace. Both wives were about ten years younger than he was. "Next time I get married, I think I'll marry a man," Bob said. " 'Cause when you get in a fight with a man, you can just hit 'im in the face."

This was his standard reply when friends asked if he was going to remarry. Bob never thought he was the problem. Both of Bob's wives had caught him with other women. The Monkey Palace was good at making money but not at keeping a marriage intact. Since his last divorce, Bob always had a girlfriend, and she was usually much younger. He never kept the same girl long.

Before Bob opened the Palace, he hired his head bartender and manager, Alphonso Sneed, a black man whose friends called him "Sugar Baby." Sugar Baby called himself Sugar Baby, too.

Only a couple of close friends knew the origin of the nickname and they weren't telling others. Sugar Baby himself never said how he got it, but it wasn't hard to discern. Unlike his boss Big Foot, Sugar Baby had a penchant for more mature girlfriends. The two men weren't the same size, either.

Sugar Baby was five nine and weighed about a hundred pounds more than Big Foot. And unlike his boss, who was clean-shaven, Sugar Baby had a well-trimmed goatee and an Afro that added three inches to his height. His 'fro looked like Dr. J's, the great basketball player. Even for those who stayed late and got drunk at the Monkey Palace, it was easy to distinguish Big Foot from Sugar Baby.

Alphonso Sneed had graduated from Monroe High School, Albany's all-black school, and was drafted into the Army, serving ten months in Vietnam. He stepped on a mine in 1968 during the Battle of Khe Sanh and severely wounded his right leg. With every step he took while mixing drinks behind a bar there was a noticeable limp.

"Shit, man, that fuckin' war was crazy," Sugar Baby said. "I knew I was goin' die over there. I just knew it the whole fuckin' time. This here limp ain't 'bout nothin'. I got the hell outta there."

Big Foot and Sugar Baby had met at the House of Jazz, a black nightclub on Highland Avenue, a few years before the Palace opened. Few white people went to the House of Jazz, but Big Foot was one of them. Sugar Baby was working the bar at the House of Jazz, sometimes selling marijuana there early in the mornings, and befriended Big Foot. Sugar Baby introduced Big Foot to a few young black girls, and the two men began partying together in both the white and black parts of Albany.

Sometimes Big Foot would drink at the bar waiting on Sugar Baby to get off work so the two could "make their rounds in the white and black worlds," they both said.

"Hell, Sugar Baby, you're my brother," Big Foot would say, as Sugar Baby nodded his head and poured his brother another glass of Jack Daniels over ice.

"That's 'cause we look just alike," Sugar Baby would say. "Had the same mommy and daddy. Ain't that right?"

When Abby and I pulled up to the Monkey Palace, the five o'clock drinking crowd was shuffling in. By ten the place would be packed and stay that way until it closed at two. Palmyra Girl was still heavy on my mind when we drove into the parking lot.

I needed to be with Abby. We sat at a table near the monkey cage and a waitress came to us. Abby ordered a glass of wine and I ordered a bottle of Budweiser. Just a few moments later she returned with our drinks.

I looked into the cage and saw that three of the monkeys were sleeping on top of one another like dominoes. The other three were pressed against each other and looked as if they were about to be asleep. Tough life, I thought. But not the life they should be living.

My first drink of beer, I consumed a third of the bottle. Abby looked at me but said nothing. We sat quietly for a few moments. Then I noticed the monkeys that hadn't been sleeping were now asleep. Tough life, I thought again. God, don't ever put me in a cage.

"John? John? John?"

I didn't say anything until she said my name a third time.

"Yeah, yeah, what is it?"

"I know what it is and you do too. It's awful. It's an awful story. An awful thing to happen. I'm sorry about it. You okay?"

"Yeah, yeah, I'm okay. She's the one not okay. Her family, wherever they are, they're not okay. I'm fine, Abby."

"You know what I mean. I'm sorry it happened. I'm just concerned about you. We live in a world where people do terrible, evil things to other people. I'm sorry about that, too."

"I know, Abby. I love you for it."

"I love you for the same reason."

She sipped her wine, and I finished my beer. The place began to fill with other after-work drinkers. Sugar Baby was serving drinks behind the bar and playing music on an eight-track tape player. The music wasn't loud, and it didn't overwhelm our conversation.

He had just inserted a tape by the Doobie Brothers, *The Captain and Me*. A new song played, called "Dark-Eyed Cajun Woman:" *I think back to the time/When I first saw your face/You were walking across the Delta/To your cold and lonely place.*

Midway through that song I saw someone who looked familiar sitting at a table on the other side of the bar, away from the dance floor. The man was sitting with Bob DuBose.

I had seen Big Foot Bob several times at his bar and at a few local parties. I had introduced him a couple of times to Abby. I could see Big Foot clearly, but the man he was with was sitting further away from me, in a darker place, and it was hard for me to identify him.

"Abby, do you see that guy sitting at that table with Big Foot? Looks like he has a suit and tie on. Do you see him?"

I nodded my head toward the table where they were. Abby looked in that direction.

"Big Foot? That's his name?"

"No, his real name is Bob DuBose. He owns the place and I've introduced you to him before."

"Okay, I remember. It was one of those keg parties on the river, I think."

"Probably. But who's that guy he's with? Looks familiar. I can't place him. If he stood up in the light I could probably figure him out."

"I'll find out. I'll be right back."

"Where you going?"

"A girl has got to go to the bathroom sometime."

Abby left and I could see her walk by the table where Big Foot and the other man were sitting. While she was away, I ordered a Crown Royal and water, and the waitress had my drink before Abby returned. I sipped and watched people come in the bar. People were dancing, others talking. Smiling and drinking. Palmyra Girl would never do any of this. I was half way through my drink when she returned.

"You ready for this?" Abby said.

"What do you got?"

She said the man with Big Foot was U.S. Senator Jefferson Beauregard Whitfield from Camilla, Georgia, about twenty-five miles south of Albany. To his friends he was known as Jeff or J.B. To some of his northern colleagues in the Senate, he was an unreconstructed Confederate. They referred to him as Senator No.

Any bill that might help people, he usually voted against. Unless it was for peanut farmers in South Georgia.

Whitfield was in his mid-forties and a descendant from a slave-owning family that had moved to South Georgia from Virginia around 1840. He had earned a law degree from the University of Georgia in the early 1970s, then returned home and practiced for a few years before winning a House seat in the Georgia legislature. He was on the move.

In 1978 he won a U.S. House seat, served two terms before leaving the Democratic Party to become a Republican in 1982, the year he was elected to the U.S. Senate. "My party has become the liberal party," Whitfield said. "It changed. I didn't."

He was elected to the Senate as a low taxes, "proud conservative and family values" candidate. He had a pretty blond wife and three young children.

"Didn't you interview him last year after the Chamber of Commerce banquet?" Abby said.

"I did. We spoke for about twenty minutes. Mickey ran the story as a feature on a Sunday."

"What was he like?"

"Like?"

"Yes, what was Senator Whitfield like? Were you impressed? I guess I read your story but I don't remember either way."

"That's why you don't remember. Nothing to be impressed about."

"Remind me then," Abby said.

I knew what she was doing. She was trying to get me to think about something other than the dead girl. I finished the Crown Royal and water and ordered another. I was drinking too fast but didn't care. Abby was still on her first glass of wine.

"It's the Reagan Revolution and he's a revolutionary. He spoke in complete sentences about the miracle of low taxes, stopping the Evil Empire and their agents down in Central America. Give the communists Nicaragua, and next thing you know, they'll take Albany. You've heard all that bullshit before."

"Didn't they say that about Vietnam in the '60s and '70s?" Abby said. "Wasn't that the Domino Theory?"

"Same shit. Same old simple bullshit. It's a simple but incorrect way to view the world. Senator No is wrong about most things, but that's probably why he won."

"What do you mean?"

I was half way through the second drink and was feeling light headed. The dance floor had cleared a bit and now I could see again Big Foot and the senator still at the table together.

"Well, he speaks like Reagan was a personal friend of Jesus. Reagan says the government is the problem. People around here eat that shit up and vote against their own self-interest. It's an old story, Abby. Don't forget family values. He said that at least ten times during the interview."

"I like it when you talk like that. I like a man with passion."

I finished the second drink and saw Big Foot leave the table. I ordered a third Crown and water, but not without a look from Abby that said she was watching my consumption. She didn't say anything.

A few minutes later, Big Foot returned to the table with two women. The women and Big Foot sat down at the table. Drinks were brought to all of them. The senator loosened his tie and leaned toward the woman sitting to his right. Big Foot put his arm around the other woman. The Doobie Brothers were still playing as three other couples came to the dance floor. Now our vision was blocked again, and we were unable to see the enator's table.

"Looks like Big Foot and Beauregard got some new friends," I said. "Pretty ones, too."

"Doesn't look like his blond-headed wife, does it? I've seen pictures of her."

"Nope. Not from here."

"How many times did he say family values during the interview?" Abby said.

"He's probably saying it now. He probably says it in his sleep."

"John, so if it's not his wife, maybe his children?"

"You know the answer to that."

"I'll be right back."

Abby again went to the bathroom and on her way there and back passed the senator's table twice. I finished my drink. The lights had now been dimmed and all the monkeys were awake. Abby was gone for about five minutes.

"Well, what did you see this time?" I said.

"They're young, John. Both of them are dark-headed and young. Both are very pretty."

"How young?"

"Eighteen, nineteen, maybe twenty."

"Doesn't sound like his wife does it? I'm sure they're not his daughters."

Abby finished her wine and reached for my right hand. The music had stopped and the dancing did too.

"Let's go, John. Leave your car here. We'll get it tomorrow. Come home with me."

"I'm ready. Let's go."

We got up to walk out of the Monkey Palace together and before we left, we both looked toward the senator's table. It was empty, but they had not gone out the front door. We would've seen them if they had. They had gone somewhere else.

CHAPTER 5

Abby's apartment was only a few minutes from the Monkey Palace and across the street from Lake Loretta, a popular spot in Albany for walkers and runners. Parents brought their children there to fish and feed the ducks. Teenage boys brought their girlfriends there to make out after the sun went down. I had done the same when I was in high school.

It was about seven o'clock when Abby drove Baby Blue into the parking lot at Shoreham Apartments. My head was fuzzy. I needed food.

The bookshelves in her living room contained a few hundred books, mostly novels and poetry. She had a few non-fiction books about southern politics and history. It was the poets she loved. She was proud to tell anyone that she organized her books by the Dewey system. A library, however small, was a sanctuary to her.

Her records were arranged in two wooden crates that had been painted red and blue. Bob Dylan dominated, but Van Morrison was close.

"They're both capable of dominion over the spirits," she said. She was addicted to words "written, spoken, and sung when done so in beauty and mystery." She would say it just the way I've written it.

"I'm going to fix us some food, John. We both need to eat. You relax. It won't take me long."

"My part will be easy."

She played Dylan's album *Blood on the Tracks* and turned the volume low as I lay down on her sofa, kicking off my shoes and putting my head on a soft white pillow she had brought from her bedroom. Thirty seconds into the first song, I was asleep. Hard sleep.

Somewhere in that hard sleep a vivid dream came to me in which I was being chased through dense trees by unrecognizable big men with long black hair. They had something in their hands but I couldn't tell what exactly. Guns maybe. There appeared to be about ten of them and they were getting closer and closer. In my sleep I made a whimpering sound as a frightened puppy would do when scared of thunder. Now I was surrounded.

"John! John! Wake up. Wake up."

Abby touched my right shoulder and shook me in a gentle way, the same way my mother did each morning getting me out of bed for school.

"Glad you're here," I said. "They were about to get me. They were getting close."

"They? Who was about to get you?"

"Whoever was after me. There was a bunch of them. They almost had me."

"Just a bad dream, John. Everybody has them. Besides, nobody's going to get you. I won't let them."

"Promise?"

"My promise is eternal, Johnny Boy. Is that long enough for you?"

Abby knelt on the floor and pressed her head against mine and wrapped her right arm over my shoulders. She stayed in that position several seconds. She kissed me three times on my cheek.

We both got up, went into her kitchen, and sat down at a black iron table with a thick glass top. All four chairs had green flowery cushions. We had pork chops, baked potato, salad, and ice tea. The food made me feel better. I forgot about the men in my dream who were chasing me. After we ate, we listened to more music and sat on the sofa and talked, but went to bed early.

Abby began reading a book by Kahlil Gibran, a Lebanese-American poet, and I kissed her good night and slept. If I did dream about being chased through the woods, I didn't remember. About thirty minutes before daylight I awoke well rested and with a clear head. I reached for her but she was gone.

Two minutes later she returned to bed naked and reached for me after getting under the sheet. We made love in a slow way. The way she liked best. Afterwards I rested my head against her black hair and could smell her living body pressed against me. My mind was still not free of the dead girl I had written about.

Abby made us coffee and toast and then, at a few minutes past seven, she drove us back to the Monkey Palace to get my car. I needed to drive to my house on North Cleveland Avenue, not far from the paper, to take a shower and get a change of clothes before going to work.

In the Palace's front parking lot there were only a couple of vehicles besides mine. One was a green Chevy van. Abby stopped next to my car. The van was parked six spaces away from us.

"If Mickey says anything tell him I'm on my way," I said. "I should be there around eight."

"You'll be on time. I know you."

"I know you, too, and that's why I love you."

She leaned over in the front seat of her car and kissed me before I got out. I watched her drive away to the newsroom. I was about to get into my car when I heard something. The side door of the van opened, making a loud screeching sound that could be heard across the Palace's parking lot. It sounded as if someone was hurting, but it was all metallic.

I turned and saw two men get out of the van. They walked toward a white Chevrolet Blazer and got inside. The van drove away and as it left I saw that both sides were fully metal and the only glass was that of the windshield. I had no clear view of the driver or of anyone sitting in the front passenger seat. But I had gotten a clear view of the two men who had exited the van and entered the Blazer.

It was Big Foot, owner of the Monkey Palace, and Senator Jefferson Beauregard Whitfield. I had seen Big Foot in the Blazer before and assumed it was his. He had gotten in the driver's side and Whitfield was in the front passenger seat. I saw no sign of the two young women they had been sitting with and buying drinks for last night at the Palace.

The two men sat inside the Blazer and appeared to be talking to one another. Three minutes later they drove out of the parking lot.

I decided to follow them, curious about where my U.S. senator, committed to family values he repeatedly said, was going after getting out of that tattered van at seven in the morning in front of the same nightclub where he was drinking with women other than his wife the night before. He probably wasn't headed to a press conference.

The Blazer pulled out of the parking lot heading north on Palmyra Road, then crossed Slappey Boulevard, still on Palmyra. They were going slow and were easy to follow. I stayed about a hundred and fifty feet behind them. There was little traffic once we passed the intersection of Slappey and Palmyra. Soon we passed the wooded area were the Palmyra Girl had been found.

There was no indication that the area was still under police investigation. I looked at the same spot where she had been covered by a white sheet. Then I looked back to the road and the white Blazer I was following.

A half-mile later the ranch-style homes gave way to row-crop fields of peanuts and corn. There were large tracks of piney woods where big white-tail deer lived and were hunted. And there were giant live oaks with Spanish moss hanging over their branches. The land was peaceful and beautiful.

The Blazer turned right on Uncle Jim's Lane, a red-dirt road that winds around the Kinchafoonee Creek. The Kinchafoonee was usually slow-moving and brown as it fed into the Flint River. Albany was founded on the Flint in the 1830s, and it became a city in which a few cotton planters became wealthy on the backs of African slaves. The planters shipped cotton south on the Flint and then on to markets in the northeast and Europe. The land and water here were marked both by beauty and tragedy.

I had been down Uncle Jim's Lane several times over the years, meeting friends along the Kinchafoonee to float on inner tubes, drink beer, and have a lot of fun on the creek. I had taken Abby with me a couple of times.

Once I took her to the Blue Hole on the creek and we swam in a spring-fed area, a place of clear, cold water. It was a hundred and five degrees in July, but that water was as cold as a January morning. God, it was refreshing. Visibility was limitless at the Blue Hole. These thoughts came to me as I drove along Uncle Jim's Lane, and now, unlike at the Blue Hole, I was having problems seeing what I wanted to see.

Thick dust rose from Uncle Jim's Lane, and I lost sight of the white Blazer. The road was full of holes. Top speed for me was ten miles an hour. A few moments later I had gotten closer to the vehicle in front of me, but it wasn't the Blazer.

Now I was behind a black Ford pickup with two large white and brown-spotted dogs in the bed. This was clear in my vision. Where was the Blazer, I thought?

There were a few houses along the way. I passed three double-wide trailers, a few smaller trailers, all sitting along the Kinchafoonee side of the road. I knew the road would dead-end in a mile or so.

I stayed behind the Ford pickup for about a quarter of a mile, then saw an opening and passed it. Now I could catch the senator and Big Foot. They had to be just up ahead.

CHAPTER 6

It looked as if the senator and Big Foot had disappeared in the Blazer. I couldn't see them anywhere.

I drove on, going slowly the whole way and did not see another vehicle as I came to the end of Uncle Jim's Lane. Where the dirt road dead-ended, I turned around and went back in the direction I had come. Still no Blazer.

They had to have pulled into one of the driveways that led to the homes along the road. On the opposite side of the road away from the homes and the Kinchafoonee were acres and acres of woods with no road access. It would be impossible to drive a Blazer in there.

Here's some other things I was a thinking about. I knew the senator's family home was down in Camilla, about thirty miles away. Plus, I knew Big Foot lived on an entirely different section of the Kinchafoonee. I had been to his house and partied there in the past. People do move from one home to another. Anything was possible.

I kept a slow ride and looked to my left at the houses and trailers along the road, and I could see the creek running smooth and peaceful behind them.

Then something along Uncle Jim's Lane caught my attention.

I stopped in front of a white double-wide that looked as if the last time it was painted the Civil War had just ended. But the big red Confederate flag that was flying in its front yard was bright and looked new. I pulled over near the mailbox that had no name on it.

I saw car tracks that led out of the white gravel driveway, through the yard and to the back of the trailer where the creek ran. The tire tracks were embedded in the green grass. I didn't see anyone or any vehicle in front of the trailer.

A light breeze fluttered the flag of President Jefferson Davis and the Confederate Army. They had fought for the Big Lie. The war is never over, I thought.

I eased my car a bit farther past the mailbox, and now I could see around the trailer to the creek where two men were standing at the water's edge. It was the senator and Big Foot. I couldn't see the Blazer, but I was certain it was back there, too.

They stood just a few feet from the brown water, and their faces were inches away from one another. They looked serious. Not relaxed and carefree as they did last night at the Monkey Palace. I could see all that from where I was parked.

I watched them for a few moments as they seemed engaged in a serious conversation with each one using his hands, chopping the air and pointing, to emphasize whatever it was he was saying. I'd seen the senator use his hands the same way during a press conference. I recalled seeing Big Foot animated in such way, but it usually involved liquor and marijuana. I couldn't rule any of that out at that moment.

I had my window down and was too far away from the men to hear what they were saying. I laid my arm across the door and leaned out trying to get the best view I could of them. Then I felt the sting. Then I heard the voice.

"You the mailman today, boy? Is that what ya are? The goddamn mailman. What ya doin' here, boy?"

With his right hand he had grabbed my left arm with force and squeezed hard, and I tried but couldn't shake away his grip. He was a powerful man. He was a big white man, six three or four and around two-hundred-and-fifty pounds. He wore a blue T-shirt under dirty blue denim overalls. His hair was black, stringy, and hung down over his eyes. The grease in it could lubricate a big car engine.

His eyes were bloodshot, and there was a two-inch scar across his chin. He was big enough to crush me. Looked mean enough to scare the shit out of most people. Me included. That's the way I felt anyway.

He kept his grip on my arm but eased the pressure some. I made no move that would've invited more force from him. This man's crazy, I thought.

"No, I'm not delivering your mail today," I said, "but you need to take your hands off me. I'm not a mailman. And I'm not your boy."

"I need to? Make me, boy. You are my *boy*. You're my purty boy."

"I'm asking you. Take your hands off me."

"You ain't nothin' but a little boy."

"Call me what you want, but I need you to let go of my arm."

"I don't care what ya need. I'll tell ya what I do when folks come 'round here. Ya ain't goin' like it."

My car was still running and I was about to press the accelerator hard and leave Big Bubba behind, but he reached over me with his left hand and snatched my keys from the ignition. He held my keys in his hand.

He was big, and now I realized he was quicker than I had guessed. He released my left arm and transferred my keys from his left hand to his right. He daggled the keys out of my reach as if it was the Big Tease.

"Ain't goin' nowhere without these, boy. Are you, boy?"

"That's right, I'm not."

He bent down over my car and was now looking at me eye-to-eye. His breath smelled of brown liquor. Lots of it, too. His crooked teeth were as brown as the liquor itself.

"Listen here, boy, I know you ain't got no mail in there," he said, "but I don't know what you doin' out here."

"It's a free country. This is not your road."

"Free? That's what you think, boy? That's a liberal-ass answer. This here is my goddamn house and my goddamn road. Ya understand me, boy? Ain't nothin' free around here unless I say so. Ya hear me?"

"I hear you."

"Now I'm gonna give ya these here keys and ya gonna drive away from here and never come back," the man said. "Like I said, I hear you. I'll never come back."

"If ya do come back, well, 'em big gators in the creek get mighty hungry. You'd be mighty tasty to them. Ya understand me, boy?"

"I understand you completely. Now can I have my keys?"

"One more thing before ya go."

"What's that?"

"Ain't nobody here but me. You ain't seen anybody but me. Got that, boy?"

"Okay, I understand. Now let me have me keys and I'll leave your property."

The big man in the overalls tossed my keys on my lap and then he backed away from my car.

"Don't forget these here big gators on the creek get mighty hungry," he said. "They'd like a young boy like you. I'm sure ya taste good."

I started my car and drove away from the man who had threatened me and from the senator and Big Foot who were standing and talking near the creek. I could still see them as I drove down Uncle Jim's Lane and back to Albany.

CHAPTER 7

At my house on North Cleveland I showered and changed clothes. It was about eight-thirty, and I was due at work thirty minutes earlier.

My arm was still sore from where Mr. Redneck had grabbed me. I didn't know his name and figured he needed one when I told Mickey and Abby why I was late. And I figured the name fit for now.

About a dozen reporters worked in the newsroom and that morning most were at their desks writing stories. Those who weren't typing were reading the morning *Chronicle*. Cigarettes and coffee and black ink and tan typing paper. Anxious energy and the First Amendment. It all had become intoxicating for me.

I walked to Mickey's desk and waited as he finished editing the last page of a story written by our reporter who covered the county commission. Thirty seconds later he placed his pencil on his desk, put the story in a wire basket, and looked at me.

"What you got, Maynard?"

"I don't know what I got."

"What kind of goddamn reporter have you become, Maynard? You either got something or you don't."

Mickey lit another Marlboro, probably number five for the morning, and leaned back in his big black leather chair. He nodded for me to sit down in the green vinyl chair in front of his desk. I did as I was instructed.

"I'll try again. What you got, Maynard?"

"Like I said, I don't know what I got but here it is."

"I'm listening."

I told Mickey about seeing the senator and Big Foot sharing a table at the Monkey Palace with a couple of young women I couldn't identify. Then I told him what I saw this morning in the Palace's parking lot and how the two men got out of a green van together, got into a white Blazer, and drove to Uncle Jim's Lane along the Kinchafoonee Creek.

My story included the white trailer that the senator and Big Foot drove behind, them standing together at that creek, and Mr. Redneck, the one who grabbed and threatened me. Mickey flipped cigarette ashes in a large glass ashtray on his desk as he listened. He drank black coffee out of a cup that said, GREEN BERET – AMERICA'S BEST. He had served in Vietnam during the war and was a decorated Green Beret.

If I had gotten too long with my story, Mickey would've said, "Don't bury the lede goddamnit." I heard that many times during the first few weeks on the job. After I finished, his reply came quick.

"Sounds like our good senator, the one of family values, may be getting a little on the side," Mickey said. "Won't be the first senator to cheat on his wife. That ain't news, Maynard. You know that. Why would I print that shit?"

"What do you know about Whitfield?"

"Probably not much more than you," Mickey said. "I've met him a couple of times. Once when he came in here to be interviewed about his support for the Contras in Nicaragua. He's a big anti-communist. Big Reagan man. Came off as a prick, though. Of course I think most of them are. You know that."

"Yeah, I do. I remember now his support for the Contras. Typical Republican position. Anti-communist, pro-family, so he says."

"So he says," Mickey said.

"Maybe he wasn't so pro-family last night at the Monkey Palace."

"So, Maynard, what the hell are you asking me?"

"I don't know what I'm asking."

"You remind me of yourself the first week on the job. Goddamnit, I thought you've learned some things since then."

"I just need a little help here, Mickey."

"Okay, what kind of help?"

"What do you know about Big Foot, Bob DuBose? The guy who owns the Monkey Palace."

"Not a damn thing other than his nickname. I don't drink there, Maynard. You know that. I drink at Madeline's, right down the street. I go to the Monkey Palace maybe once a year. Maybe."

Mickey had his personal table and regular drinking buddies at Madeline's Bar on Pine Avenue, a short walk from the paper. Lawyers, young and old, local politicians, and business men drank at Madeline's, day and night. If you wanted the gossip in Albany, true or false, that's where you went.

"I understand."

"What do you know about him, Maynard?"

"A little bit. I've talked to him a few times at parties out on the Flint River. And a few times at the Palace. He was in the military. Likes to party and seems to be making money from his bar, just based on the crowds I see. He's been married but he's divorced now. He likes young women."

"He likes young women, you say. Well, I'll be damned. He's got that in common with ten thousand other men in Albany his age."

"You're probably right," I said.

"How young?"

"What?"

"You said he likes young girls. Girls that are thirteen or twenty?"

"More like twenty."

"That's not a story, Maynard. That's not a crime."

"Should I follow up on what I saw last night and this morning?" I said.

"What the hell do you think you saw besides two men having drinks with two women? One of the men happens to be a U.S. senator. So? That shit happens every day. That's not a story, goddamnit. There's nothing there to print."

"What about the big guy who grabbed me? Mr. Redneck."

"What about him?"

"He didn't want me to be there. He didn't want me to see what I was seeing. And I was seeing the senator and Big Foot."

"Hell, I don't know," Mickey said. "Maybe he made the arrangements to get the women. Maybe you pissed him off. Still not a story. A redneck with liquor on his breath grabbed you in front of a Confederate flag. That's all you got? Shit, it happens every day around here."

"Yeah, I pissed him off all right. He didn't want me there."

"Hell, there's no story when a politician cheats on his wife," Mickey said. "That's not the public's business unless he's paying for it. Prostitution is illegal in this state."

"Okay, what should I do about all of this?"

"Anything else on the girl's body they found off Palmyra Road?"

"No, but I'm going to follow up. I'm staying on it."

"Good, I want you to. In the meantime, if you want to ask the senator and Big Foot what they were doing besides screwing women, I'll leave that up to you. If you find something, I want to know. Maybe there's something there, maybe not. Got it?"

"Will do, Mickey."

He picked up his black telephone's receiver and began making a call. I walked to Abby's desk where she was rewriting a press release from the city commission. I sat down in a chair in front of her desk but didn't say anything. She was focused on her work and didn't look at me. Two minutes later she scrolled the tan typing paper from her typewriter, placed it on her desk, and turned to look at me.

"Well, Johnny Boy, did Mickey give you a good cussing out for being late for work?"

"It never came up. Besides, he'll give you a good cussing for being on time. That's Mickey."

"You're living a charmed life, Johnny Boy, but it's not like you to be late for anything. It's been that way since I've known you. What was it you told me your dad said about such things?"

"If you're on time, you're late. Whatever you're doing, make it important. Get there early."

"Good advice. He served in the Air Force in the late 1940s, right?"

"Sure did. Military training I guess. But he said it a lot when I was a kid."

"So what's your excuse this morning? Spent the night with a pretty girl who loves you? Is that it, Johnny Boy?"

"More to it than that."

"Okay, I'm listening. Go ahead."

She leaned back in her chair much the same way Mickey had done when I told him my story. I gave Abby the same version. Then I stopped and waited.

"I do remember the green van this morning when I dropped you off," Abby said. "But I didn't see a white Blazer. At least I don't think I did."

"It was on the other side of the van. I was able to see it once I got out of your car. You had a bad angle. I saw the senator and Big Foot get into the Blazer. Nobody else was with them."

"Okay, let me get this straight. You see them get in the Blazer and leave the Monkey Palace and you decide to follow them. Why?"

"Abby, I don't know. I just thought it was odd. We had seen them the night before and they were still together. Don't you think that's odd?"

"What's odd to me is that you followed them all the way to the Kinchafoonee Creek," she said. "Now that's odd. Do you want to be in some spy novel, Johnny Boy? That's what this sounds like to me. Maybe work for the CIA. I've probably said that to you before."

"Are you making fun of me?"

"Maybe."

"Oh, you're so funny. You're so funny, Abby."

"Let me be sure I have this. When you leave Uncle Jim's Lane to come to work, they are standing together behind a trailer along the creek. Did I get this right? The senator and Big Foot together."

"Right. Just like I said."

"The other guy. You called him Mr. Redneck?"

"Not to his face. I wouldn't have done that. He said he'd feed me to the gators if I ever came back. Abby, I believed him. I never got his name. Never asked."

"Sounds like a nice guy."

"Just your type, Abby."

"I bet he reads Whitman and Mark Twain."

"More likely he drinks Jack Daniels and chews Red Man."

"He grabbed your arm, took your keys, and threatened you?" Abby said.

"Yeah, that's right. You paid attention to my story. Thought he was going to beat the shit out of me in front of his giant Confederate flag."

"Confederate flag?" Abby said. "You left that part out."

"Yeah, it was a big one in front of his trailer. Would've made Jefferson Davis proud."

"Probably made Senator Whitfield proud, too."

"Probably did."

"So what's next? What did Mickey say?"

"He left it up to me, and I'm going back to the Monkey Palace to see what I can see."

"When?"

"Tonight. You want to go?"

"I probably need to go to look after you."

"Why?"

"There may be somebody there who wants to feed you to the gators."

"You're a funny girl, Abby. A real funny girl."

CHAPTER 8

At about seven that evening I picked up Abby at her apartment and we drove to the Monkey Palace.

We sat at the same table we had used the previous night. A waitress came by and asked us what we wanted. White wine for Abby, a Budweiser for me.

At the same table where Big Foot and the senator had been the night before, there were four women, all appeared to be in their mid-to-late twenties. They were drinking and laughing and looking for what the Monkey Palace had to offer. A man about their age walked past them, and they inspected him as if they were farmers buying cattle at an auction. It was the Monkey Palace inspection. Both men and women used it.

"Well, Mr. CIA agent, do you see them?" Abby said. "Maybe they're both working for the Soviet Union. Now that would be a prize-winning story, Johnny Boy. Maybe a Pulitzer."

"See who? I don't know what you're talking about. I work for the *Chronicle*, not the *New York Times*."

"Oh, now you think you're so clever. Do you see Big Leg, I mean Big Foot, and your senator? The ones you been spying on."

"He's your senator, too. Represents everyone in the state. And I wasn't spying, Abby. I followed them in my car. That's all."

"Sounds like spying to me."

"I don't see either one of them right now," I said. "I'm looking, but I don't see them."

The waitress returned with our drinks, I paid her and she left to wait on the table next to us. The place was filling up.

"Well, Johnny Boy, let's toast to your new job with the CIA. We're going to miss you at the paper."

She raised her wine glass over our table, I tapped it with my beer bottle and we both drank.

"Okay, I'll play your little game," I said. "If you want me to be a spy, I will. Anything for you, my love. I'll be the best spy ever. You can count on it."

At that moment I looked toward the bar and saw Sugar Baby, the bartender, serve a drink to a familiar-looking man who had just sat down. It took me just another moment to realize I knew who he was, but I didn't know his name.

It was the sonofabitch who had grabbed me that morning when I was parked along Uncle Jim's Lane watching the senator and Big Foot talking along the creek. The same man that snatched my keys from the ignition. The same one who said if ever saw me again at the creek, he'd feed me to the alligators. Hard to forget a meeting like that.

"That's, him, Abby," I said, as I nodded toward the bar.

"That's who?"

"That's the man I saw this morning at the creek. Same place I followed the senator and Big Foot. I told you about him. He grabbed me and my keys. Threatened to feed me to the gators. We hit it off well. His name is Mr. Redneck, for now anyway."

"Great name, Johnny Boy. Your new best friend?"

"I think so."

She looked at the bar, back at me, and then at the bar again.

"Well, did he follow us here, or did we follow him?" Abby said. "You're with the CIA now. What do you think?"

"Doesn't matter now. What matters is that he's here, and maybe Big Foot and the senator are, too. Maybe they're together again like they were last night."

"Oh, John, so what? Where's the story? A nightclub owner and a U. S. senator are having drinks. That's your story? That's no story. Isn't that what Mickey said?"

"Maybe there's no story but maybe there is. Mickey doesn't know everything."

"So, what are you going to do if you see them here together to-night? Going to join them for drinks? Ask them if they're sleeping with young girls? Ask them what kind of criminal activity they're up to? What's your plan, Johnny Boy?"

"I'll think of something, Abby. Don't forget I'm a spy. A damn clever one, too. And you ain't much help."

"Funny, funny, funny. Oh, my Johnny Boy is a funny spy."

I noticed that the seat next to Mr. Redneck was empty. He had finished his drink with three big gulps and had ordered another. I knew where I was going.

"I'll only be a couple of minutes," I said. "I've got some spying to do."

I got up from our table to walk to the bar but stood by Abby for a moment. She placed her hand on my arm.

"Be careful, John. Just be careful."

"I'll be all right. No gators in here to feed me to. Monkeys eat pea-nuts, not reporters. I'll be right back. Just got a couple of questions for him. He's a friend of mine, remember?"

I walked to the bar and took the seat next to Mr. Redneck. He was staring into his drink as if he was looking for something important he had lost. I sat down next to him. From behind the bar, Sugar Baby approached me.

"Whatta you have, my man?"

"A bottle of Bud, please," I said.

"It's on the way," Sugar Baby said.

When the man I sat next to heard my voice, he looked at me with squinted eyes as if he was struggling to focus. He was either drunk from the liquor or pissed off at me. Probably both, I thought.

"Boy, is that ya again, boy?"

"I didn't get a chance to introduce myself to you this morning. I'm John Maynard, and I work for the *Albany Chronicle*. What's your name?"

"I ain't gotta name. My mama never gave me one. If I did have a name, I wouldn't tell. Now git away from me and this here bar, you hear."

Sugar Baby sat a bottle of beer in front of me. I paid him for it and tipped him.

"Thanks, my man. Need anything else here? If you do, just holler. I'll take care of ya. We take good care of everybody at the Palace."

"We're all good," I said. "Thanks for the beer."

"Coldest in town," Sugar Baby said.

He walked away to wait on other customers as an eight-track tape recording of the Spinners was playing a song called "Rubberband Man:" *Rubberband Man starts to jam/Movin' up and down across the land/Got people all in his ways/Everything about him seems outta place.*

Several couples were dancing. The Spinners had gotten them out of their seats and onto the dance floor.

I turned to look at Abby sipping her wine and sitting alone. She saw me do so and smiled and nodded her head. I focused again on the man I had come to question.

"I told you my name," I said, "why won't you tell me yours? I just want to know your name."

I extended my right hand to shake his, but I knew he wouldn't do it. I figured at the bar, in front of all these people, I was safe.

"If ya don't git ya hand out of my face, I'll cut if off with the knife I'm carryin' in my pocket. Ya understand me, boy? I guess ya just don't understand nothin'. Stubborn boys like you git hurt. Real bad hurt."

"Some people say I'm stubborn. I guess it's my line of work. I don't mean to be stubborn, though. I really don't care what people say, but I just want to talk to you for a minute."

"Bet ya care if I cut ya hand off," he said. "Ya won't be so stubborn after that. Might cut ya little dick off, too. Wait and see, boy."

"Look, if you don't want to tell me your name, I understand. I just want to know what my senator, the one who represents you and all the other people of Georgia, was doing here last night and at the creek this morning."

"I done told ya to git away from me. I done told ya. Ain't gonna say nothin' else to ya. Ya say another word to me, I'll pull this here knife outta my pocket. I don't give a goddamn-shit who sees me do it."

He's not going to do anything to me at the bar at the Monkey Palace, I thought. I couldn't be sure of that if it was just the two of us at that trailer on the creek.

"Do you live at that trailer where I saw you this morning?"

He then reached for me and grabbed the collar of my light blue shirt underneath my chin and pulled me to him. I was six inches from his face.

"Looky here, boy, ya need to git away from me with your questions. Ya must not like livin'."

His familiar breath was of liquor, the whites of his eyes were red, and he still hadn't washed his greasy black hair. He tightened his grip on me. The man was strong.

Out of the corner of my eye, I could see Sugar Baby walking toward us.

"Everything okay here?" Sugar Baby said. "Want another drink?"

The man I called Mr. Redneck released his grip on me. I eased back fully into the barstool.

"Just talking things over," I said. "And I think we've got it all worked out now."

"You're a lucky piece of shit," the man said. "If I had ya in the parking lot, I'd rip ya arm off and feed it to the goddamn buzzards."

"Not the gators?"

"I'd give 'em some, too."

I took a drink of my beer and looked at Abby again. One of her friends had stopped at our table to say hello to her, and she had not seen the man grab me. Good, I thought.

"So you're not going to answer my question about the senator and Big Foot?"

"Go to hell, boy. And when you git there, stay there. I hope it burns ya ass up. And the rest of ya, too."

The man got up from the barstool, left a ten on the bar, and walked toward the back of the Palace. A few seconds after he left, I followed him. I didn't see him at a table. I checked the bathroom and he wasn't there.

I opened the backdoor of the bar that led to the ally and a few parking spaces for vehicles. I didn't see him.

What I did see was a green van driving away from the Palace. It looked to be the same one I had seen that morning. The one the senator and Big Foot had gotten out of before getting into the white Blazer.

CHAPTER 9

When the van was out of sight, I returned to the Monkey Palace and took the same seat at the bar I had just left. Maybe Sugar Baby could help me.

Abby's friend was still visiting her, so I decided to ask Sugar Baby a few questions. He probably wouldn't threaten to cut my arm off. Or cut my dick off. Or feed me to the gators.

He saw me take the same barstool I had left and walked over to me. He picked up Mr. Redneck's empty glass and wiped the black-wooden bar with a white towel.

"Need another beer, my man?"

"No, I'm good for now. Thanks. But I do have a question for you, if you don't mind."

"I answer 'em all night. Got some good ones of my own, too. Whatta you need, my man?"

"Who was that man who just left? The one I was talking with. He wouldn't tell me his name."

"That was Pearl. He don't say much to anybody. Most people don't want to talk to 'im anyhow. You probably figured that out by now."

"Pearl?"

"That's what I said."

"Does he have a real name?"

"That one's real. That's the only one I know."

"Is he friends with Big Foot?"

"Ain't gonna say friends. They know each other. But Big Foot knows everybody. Those that he doesn't, well, they know him."

"What can you tell me about Pearl? What does he do for a living?"

"We're past one question now, aren't we?"

"Yeah, but I figured you wouldn't mind," I said. "Where does he work? Pearl, that is."

"Don't know but I never asked. Like I said, he ain't the talkin' type. Lots of people come in the Palace and love to talk. Not him."

"Does he come in a lot?"

"What number question is that?"

"I'm not counting."

"I see 'im regular. Once or twice a week or so. He drinks Jack Daniels. Drinks 'em fast. Sometimes five or six at one setting. He's always alone, too. Sits at the same place each time. If he comes in and sees someone sitting there, he turns and walks out. Pearl got his ways."

"Ever seen Big Foot drink with him?"

"Maybe. Don't 'member for sure."

"Does he live on the Kincafoonee Creek?"

"Was it one question or one hundred?"

"I don't remember what I said. But do you know where Pearl lives?"

"Don't know. Could be the creek. Now tell me why you got all these questions. I saw Pearl grab you. What you two arguin' 'bout? Don't you know he could kill you?"

"No argument. I just had a few questions for him and he didn't like it. That's all."

"I've seen you in here before. What's your name?"

"John Maynard."

"Same one that's in the paper?"

"Same one," I said. "That's me. I write for the *Albany Chronicle.*"

"I saw your story about the dead girl they found on Palmyra," Sugar Baby said. "Who'd do such terrible thing? Breaks your heart, man. Got some mean people in this town. Have they arrested the guy yet?"

"What guy?"

"The guy who killed that little girl."

"No, there hasn't been anyone arrested yet," I said.

"God, whoever did that, well, they need to do the same to him."

"We'll see. I'm staying on the story. As soon as there's an arrest made, I'll report it. Yeah, it's an awful story."

"You ain't just curious about Pearl, then. You workin' on a story about 'im, too, aren't ya? What'd he do? What's the story?"

"Right now nothing. Just don't know yet."

"If you writin' a story 'bout Pearl, who'd want to read that?"

"Maybe no one. Got another question for you."

"You don't know how to count, do ya?"

"Is your boss friends with Senator Jefferson Beauregard Whitfield?"

"Who?"

"Our U.S. senator. The one from Camilla. I saw him in here last night sitting with Big Foot. They were having drinks with a couple of women."

"Oh, you mean J.B. That's what Big Foot calls him anyway. They may be friends, maybe not. Yeah, J.B. was in here last night. That's right. I 'member now."

"Do they see each other a lot?"

"You must be writin' a story 'bout 'em."

"No, like I said, just curious."

"I don't believe ya."

"It's the truth. Right now, anyway."

"They ain't friends, no sir. I wouldn't say that."

"What are they then? Business associates? They chase women together? Drinking buddies? What's the relationship?"

"That's a heap more than one question, my man. The only thing I can say, is that J.B. comes in every now and then and Big Foot buys him a drink. Don't know more than that. I don't ask. Know whatta I mean?"

"Yeah, I know what you mean."

Sugar Baby turned from me and pulled a Budweiser from the cooler behind the bar. He popped the top and set the bottle in front of me.

"This here's on me," Sugar Baby said. "You must be mighty thirsty after askin' that one question. The Palace is getting busy. Just like always."

"Thanks, Sugar Baby."

"You mighty welcome, my man."

He turned from me to wait on two young women who had taken seats next to me at the bar. They were both blonds with heavy makeup and heavy jewelry. I could smell their perfume before they sat down.

If they smiled any harder, their faces would likely crack. They had the hungry Monkey Palace look in their eyes. It was inspection time. They looked at me, and I knew I needed to leave the bar.

I took the beer Sugar Baby had given me and returned to the table where Abby was waiting on me. Her friend who had stopped by to visit was now dancing with her boyfriend. Abby saw me walking across the club toward her, and she smiled big.

I took my seat again at the table, and the waitress returned with another glass of wine for her. All the tables were full now. They would remain that way until the Palace closed. The real monkeys didn't seem to mind, as I looked at them in their cage, a few sleeping and a few eating peanuts. Life was always the same for them.

I kept looking for the senator and Big Foot. I wondered if they had driven away in the green van with Pearl. Two great names, I thought. Big Foot and Pearl.

"So, Mr. Spy, Mr. Big Time Spy, what did you learn from your new friend?" Abby said.

"Oh, we're still close. I'd say closer than ever. He really likes me, Abby. This time he grabbed me by my shirt and pulled me in his face and threatened me. Same bad breath from this morning."

"John, this is not funny anymore. You need to be careful. You need to stay away from that guy. There are crazy people in this world. Crazy and violent. The world can be a crazy place."

"Who said that? Was it Whitman? Blake? Maybe Yeats? I know it was one of those poets you love reading. You love them more than you love me."

"No, *I said that*. About the poets, that's a different kind of love."

"I asked him a question, that's all," I said. "The same thing we do every day."

"Well, did you get any useful information out of him?"

"Yeah, sure did."

"What was it?"

"Said if I didn't stop asking questions, he was going to take the knife out of his pocket and cut my arm off. Just one arm. Not both. And he said he'd cut my dick off."

"What's his name?"

"Pearl."

"What did you say?"

"He wouldn't even tell me his name. But Sugar Baby told me he goes by Pearl. Sugar Baby said that's his real name, Pearl. And he knows everybody that comes in here."

"Who's Sugar Baby?" Abby said.

"He's the bartender. At least he answered my questions. And gave me a cold one on the house."

I took a drink from my beer and Abby sipped her wine. We both looked around the Monkey Palace as if any second now someone would be arriving that we had been waiting on.

"Sugar Baby, Big Foot, and Pearl. What kind of story is this, John?"

"I don't know. Nothing maybe."

"Well, did you learn anything about Big Foot and the senator from your bartender?"

"According to Sugar Baby, the senator comes in here from time to time and has drinks with Big Foot. That's all he told me."

"You think Sugar Baby knows more than he's saying?"

"Probably. He's a bartender. He hears a lot. He sees a lot."

"Where is Pearl? I don't see him at the bar."

"He left, Abby. He went out the back way."

"Was he alone when he left?"

"As far as I could tell."

"Good. There doesn't seem to be a story here anyway."

"Abby, I followed him out the backdoor and saw him drive away."

"Why did you do that?"

"I'm glad I did. I saw him drive off in the same green van that the senator and Big Foot got out of this morning when you dropped me off."

"You sure about that?"

"Of course I'm sure. I'm a trained spy for the CIA. Remember?"

"Not funny, John. Not funny."

CHAPTER 10

Senator Whitfield saw the girl looking at him. She was young, had dark hair, dark skin, and a smile of innocence and beauty. He wanted what he saw. There were others like her. They worked the brothels and hotels outside of Palmerola, a U. S. air base in Honduras.

He had flown to the base in the spring of 1983, just a few months after he was sworn in as the junior U. S. senator from Georgia. After his election the previous November, he had asked for and received an appointment to the powerful Senate Armed Services Committee.

Like other Republicans during that period, he had expressed concern, if not fear, of the threat of communism coming out of Central America and spreading to the United States. Whether he believed it or not, it was an old political theme that still helped politicians get elected.

"The communists down there have to be stopped," Whitfield had told newspaper reporters. "It represents a cancer right here on our land mass. We must destroy the cancer before it spreads."

That kind of talking helped him get elected. He used the statement several times during the campaign and again when he joined the Armed Services Committee. "Communism in Central America is a threat to freedom in the United States and peace itself." He said that many times, too.

Whitfield had flown to Palmerola, five miles from the city of Comayagua, on a C-47 U. S. military cargo plane. He made the flight from Ft. Benning, a U. S. Army Base in Columbus, Georgia. He joined twenty members of the Georgia National Guard who had been assigned to the base for six months. There were already twenty-five members of the same unit who had arrived at Palmerola a few weeks earlier.

The freshman senator had asked the military for permission to travel to Honduras for a fact-finding tour of the U. S. government's efforts to stop communism in Central America. He approached the five-day trip with the zeal of an early Christian missionary. He said U. S. policy there had to be maintained.

What he did not know when he left Ft. Benning was that he would approach the young prostitutes in Honduras with the same kind of anti-communism zeal he had brought to the Senate. International travel has a way of expanding one's horizons.

He visited prostitutes each night he was at the base, but he also called his wife each night and asked about her wellbeing and that of their two children. He didn't talk long. He was busy helping his country.

Since 1981, Palmerola represented the base of operations of the U. S. government in its efforts to support a group known as the Contras, who were fighting to overthrow Nicaragua's government. For many years, the United States had backed the ruthless Samoza family that ruled Nicaragua until 1979. During that year, a revolutionary government known as Sandinistas came to power.

This communist-leaning government ignited fear among many in the United States, including Senator Whitfield. The "cancer" that Whitfield spoke about was the Sandinistas movement.

Whitfield had gone to Honduras in the hopes that the cancer was being defeated. As for the prostitutes, well, he was willing to do whatever it took to fight communism.

Hundreds of U. S. personnel had been assigned to the base during the months preceding Whitfield's arrival. This included Special Forces, the Air Force, and the National Guard. They assisted the Contras as they conducted military attacks deep inside neighboring Nicaragua.

Whitfield knew all of this before he boarded the C-47 at Ft. Benning, but what he didn't know was the extent of the impoverished living conditions endured by most Hondurans. He saw it up close. Nor did he know, until the day he arrived, how cheap it was to buy a teenage prostitute.

He had never paid for sex in the United States. Never even thought about it, he said later. Been married for several years and never cheated on his wife once. That changed in Honduras.

His first night at Palmerola, he borrowed a jeep from one of the officers with the Georgia National Guard. It was about six when he left the base alone and drove into Comayagua, a city of around a hundred thousand residents. Once inside the city, he saw children, some looked to be seven or eight, begging for food and money. There were many of them.

He saw what appeared to be young prostitutes positioning themselves near the Hotel Maya. He had heard from other politicians that the Maya was one of the better hotels in the city. He had chosen, though, to spend the nights at the base in the officers' quarters. He kept looking at the prostitutes. There were eight or ten of them on the streets around the hotel.

He parked his jeep near the hotel. He had not planned this but it played out this way. He walked into the hotel. He was wearing khakis, a green T-shirt, and a light leather jacket. Nothing about the outfit said U. S. senator.

He paid eight dollars for the room and walked back outside and paid five dollars for one of the girls he had passed. She was maybe sixteen, but maybe not.

She only knew a little English but said this like she had done so many times: "Show me what you like. I do for you. I love America. I love you."

The senator and the girl spent an hour together in room 141 at the Hotel Maya. He tipped her a dollar when she left. No one knew him. No one would find out what he had done. It all seemed too easy and it felt right.

Five minutes after she left the room, he did the same and drove back to the base. It was approaching nine o'clock, and the night air was cool, the moon rising high. He felt good. So far, he was enjoying his fact-finding trip to Honduras. He was serving his country.

A half-mile from the base was a bar called Cowboy Heaven, a place where U. S. personnel drank, played cards, and sometimes solicited prostitutes. Whitfield decided to stop at the bar and speak with some of the men about efforts to help the Contras. He had gone down there for that.

The place had about fifteen tables and a dozen or so seats at the bar. All the employees wore black or tan cowboy hats and cowboy boots. There were pictures of John Wayne and Roy Rogers and Ronald Reagan on the walls. A singer was singing Willie Nelson songs. The place was almost full and there were several women moving from table to table looking for business. Cowboy Heaven. Perfect name.

Whitfield took a seat at the bar and ordered a Salva Vida, a popular Honduran beer. He had a smile on his face, and one on the inside, from the time he spent at the Hotel Maya. No remorse. No regret.

Three seats to his right, a man was sitting and drinking alone. From his uniform, Whitfield could tell he was part of the Georgia National Guard. A pearl-handled gun was strapped to the man's waist. He didn't recognize the man as being on the C-47 that Whitfield flew in on. The man appeared to be in his early thirties and was drinking Jack Daniels.

"Excuse me, can I ask you a question?" Whitfield said.

"Yeah, go ahead, but I might not answer it. You the bigshot senator, right?"

"Maybe not a bigshot, but I am a senator from Georgia. I'd like to talk to you for a few minutes, if I could. I want to know how things are going down here."

"Don't want to talk. Never liked answering questions. That's why I dropped out of school in the seventh grade. Talk to somebody else."

"Will you talk to me if I buy you a drink?" Whitfield said.

"One drink. One question."

The man's glass was half full, but he downed the rest of it and looked at the senator.

"What are you drinking?" Whitfield said.

"Jack and ice. Mostly Jack."

Whitfield motioned for the bartender in the black cowboy hat and black vest and ordered the drink. The man from the Georgia National Guard took the fresh glass of Jack and downed a third of it.

"I'm Senator Jefferson Whitfield, and I just flew in today from Ft. Benning. Like I said, I'm down here to find out how things are going. How long you been here?"

"Near 'bout three months."

"How are things going?"

"What things ya talkin' 'bout?"

"Our work with stopping the communists and helping the Contras retake their country. How do you think we're doing?"

"Ya want me to tell ya how thing are goin' down here? Is that what ya want?"

"Yes, I do."

"Ya should already know that. Ya and the rest of the pretty suits up there in D. C. Ya know everything, don't ya?"

"I'm up there, you're down here," Whitfield said. "I just want to know if you think our side is winning."

"Winning? Is that what ya said?"

"Yes, winning."

"Them Contras ya like so much, they blow up schools, rape young girls, and torture teenage boys. Winning? Ya think that's winning? Ya think that's how ya stop communism?"

The man took another long drink from his Jack Daniels, set the empty glass on the bar. He then motioned for the bartender to bring him another one.

"Is there anything good happening down here? We're spending millions of dollars on this policy. Can you tell me something good?"

"Yeah, I reckon."

The man took a long drink of his fresh Jack Daniels. Took out a pack of Camels from his shirt pocket, lit one with a gray metallic flip-top lighter and took a long pull. He blew the smoke toward the bartender in the black cowboy hat.

"Liquor and prostitutes are cheap," the man said. "That's somethin' good. Somethin' *real* good. Ain't it?"

"That's not exactly why our government, in your name and mine, is supporting the Contras."

"Try tellin' that to the men I'm with in the Georgia National Guard.

They'd believe me before they believed ya. In your name and mine."

"Our purpose here is a noble one," Whitfield said. "We're here to stop the spread of communism. To give freedom to the people of Nicaragua. If the communists take Central America, we could be next."

"Save that bullshit for ya voters in Georgia."

"What I said is the truth."

"No, I'll tell ya the truth one more time" the man said. "Cheap liquor and cheap prostitutes. That's why we're here. I reckon you know that by now. Don't ya?"

"I just got here today. I'm only going to be here a few days. I want to learn as much as I can before I report to my committee. I'm on the Armed Services Committee."

"Committee? Must've had the first meeting at the Hotel Maya."

"Well, no. I didn't have a meeting there, but I did drive by it earlier this evening. I borrowed a jeep and wanted to see the area around the base. That's all."

"I guess ya can say it that way, if you wanna. If it makes ya feel better. Maybe ya gotta a wife back in Georgia. Some kids even. Maybe you're a deacon in ya church. Wouldn't surprise me."

"I'm married and have two children. And, yes, I am a deacon in the First Baptist Church in Camilla, Georgia. Proud of all of that."

"Sure ya are, Senator Whitfield."

"I'm not here to talk about my family. I'm here to learn about our operations from this base into Nicaragua."

"What did you learn at the Hotel Maya? How did you like room 141?"

Whitfield was taking a drink of his Salva Vida when he heard the man say "room 141." He looked as if he was going to choke on the Honduran beer. Best beer in the country, most people said.

"I saw the hotel. I don't know anything about room 141. I never went inside. I just drove past it."

"You're a fine liar. Ya gonna be a great senator. Our country's gonna be proud of ya. Maybe even president one day you keep lyin' like that."

"I'm not lying," Whitfield said. "I didn't go into that hotel. I just drove by it."

"Let's see if you 'member this: 'Show me what you like, and I'll do it for you. I love Americans. I love you.' That sure is a purty thing to say. Ain't it?"

After the man said the exact same thing the young prostitute had said to Whitfield, he finished his drink and got up from the barstool. He was headed out the door and back to the barracks on base.

"I'll be here tomorrow night," the man said. "Buy me another drink, and we can talk some more."

Senator Whitfield said nothing as the man left Cowboy Heaven. He looked at the bartender in the black cowboy hat and ordered another drink.

Jack Daniels straight this time.

CHAPTER 11

The next morning after trying to talk with Pearl at the Monkey Palace, I called Detective McGill and asked if there were any new developments in the case of the Palmyra Girl.

He said he had nothing of significance to report but did confirm that the Georgia Bureau of Investigation had sent a couple of agents from Cordele, about forty miles east of Albany, to assist in the investigation. The agents were already working the case. I told him I would continue to follow the story.

After speaking with McGill, I told Mickey about my conversation, if you could call it that, with Pearl in an attempt to learn about the connection between Senator Whitfield and Big Foot.

I also told him about what Sugar Baby told me concerning the relationship between Big Foot and our senator.

"Jesus Christ, Maynard! What kind of story is this? If you even have a story and I don't think you do. Big Foot, Sugar Baby, and Pearl. Are you a newspaper reporter or do you write comic books?"

"Mickey, I don't know if I have a story, either. Don't you think it's strange that Pearl threatened me twice just because I had a couple of questions about Big Foot and Whitfield?"

"Strange? Goddamnit, there's a lot of strange shit happening. Every day. Doesn't mean it's a news story. Maybe the guy's an around-the-clock asshole. Some guys are just that way. Shit, this place is full of rednecks."

"Yeah, maybe so."

"What are you working on today? Did you follow up with the young girl they found? Anything new there?"

"Nothing. I made a call earlier."

"Check in with the cops every day. Stay on it."

"Mickey, I don't have anything right now," I said. "Is it okay with you if I drive back to the creek just to look around?"

"Look around for what, goddamnit? Somebody else with a crazy-ass name? Someone called Jelly Belly, Shit Face or maybe Pea Brain. Those are all good sources, don't you think?"

"I think they're all great sources. I can't wait to interview them. I don't have anything else working right now, Mickey."

"I thought you'd like them," Mickey said. "If you think there might be a story out there on the creek or the Monkey Palace or God knows where, go ahead, Maynard. Stay away from Pearly."

"It's Pearl."

"Him too."

"I'll stay away from him, I promise. Just going to drive through and take a look at things along the creek."

"All right. Get going then."

I left Mickey's desk and spoke to Abby as she was working on a feature story about summer activities for school children offered by the Albany Recreation Department. She said the same thing Mickey said.

"John, just promise me one thing."

"I know what it is. It's a promise."

"Good. Look around out there if you want, but stay away from your new friend, Pearl."

"If he threw me in the creek, would you rescue me from the gators, Abby?"

"No, you've been warned. You are on your own with the gators. I'm not in the rescuing business."

"You don't love me anymore?"

"I do love you, Johnny Boy, but there are limits."

"You're making me sad, now."

"Come back to me, and I'll make you happy later."

"Good deal. Sounds like a real good deal."

I drove away from the newsroom with the sun turning from warm to hot. I had a couple of pens, my notepad, and a Nikon camera. I figured that was all I needed to contend with any gator if Pearl tossed me into the creek. He was plenty big enough to do it. I had seen some gators in the Kinchafoonee Creek and on the nearby Flint River that were as long as my car. Pearl probably knew them all by name.

When I turned north on Palmyra Road and was about to pass the wooded area where the girl had been found, I saw a boy lying on a dirt road. The same road that had led to the girl's body. Next to the boy, probably eleven or twelve, was a red Schwinn bicycle with high handlebars. And next to the bike was a long gun. I couldn't tell if the gun was real or a toy. I thought the boy was hurt.

I turned onto the dirt road and stopped near him. He was slender but his muscles were taunt. He was a white boy with tanned skin from spending a lot of time outdoors. I got out of my car to check on him.

"Are you all right?" I said. "You need some help?"

"No, dang it, I don't need any help. I just missed him. Barely missed him. He was a big un. Dang it, I can't stand it when I miss 'em!"

"Missed what?"

"That squirrel, dang it. The biggest I've ever seen. Bigger than my dog, Rusty. He's a cocker. Biggest squirrel in Georgia, maybe the whole world."

Three squirrel tails were tied to the boy's handlebars, and on the back of his white seat there was a rattle that had been cut off a rattlesnake. The rattle was a couple of inches long. Must've been a big, big snake, I thought, maybe five or six feet long.

"What squirrel? I don't see a squirrel."

"He's gone now," the boy said. "Probably ran up that big pine over yonder. Saw him headed that way when I missed 'im. Dang it!"

The boy pointed to a large pine tree, no more than fifty feet from where the body had been discovered. The tree towered above others in the dense thicket.

He got himself off the ground and brushed dirt from his shorts that had once been a long pair of jeans. He was bare-footed, wore a wrinkled white T-shirt, and a blue ball cap with no marking.

Both knees were bleeding, and he rubbed the blood off with his hands. He didn't say a word about the blood. Tough kid, I thought.

"Can I help you?"

"Nah, I said I'm okay."

He picked his bike up and his gun. He stood by his bike looking at the pine tree where the squirrel had run. I looked that way too and didn't see a squirrel or any other animal the boy might shoot.

"What kind of gun you got there?" I said.

"Just a regular 'ol pellet gun. My daddy won't let me bring my twenty-two over here. Says there are too many people around here. Might shoot somebody and not mean it. But dang it, Daddy knows I'm a good shot. I only shoot what I want to shoot. That's how my daddy taught me."

"So you shoot squirrels over here," I said. "You eat them?"

"Yep, my pa pa cooks 'em. Gravy, too. It ain't my favorite. I like best the gator tails. That's my favorite. Squirrels are okay."

"So your granddad cooks alligators?"

"That's what I said."

"Where's he get the gators?"

"Ain't from no grocery store," the boy said. "Creek is right over yonder. River ain't much farther. You from 'round here? You should know that."

"Yeah, I live in Albany."

I thought about Pearl for a moment and his threat to feed *me* to the gators. And I remembered I once ate gator tail at a party on the river when I was in college. It tasted good.

"What caused you to wreck your bike?"

"You ever seen John Wayne ride a horse and shoot a bad guy on TV?"

"A few times," I said.

"That's what I was doin'. Had both hands on my gun and no hands on my bike. I was haulin' it. Had the squirrel on the run. They faster than gators, you know."

"So what happened? What caused it?"

"That there bottle. That one right there."

The boy pointed to the dirt road and what looked to be an empty liquor bottle. I looked closer and saw it was a pint of Jack Daniels.

"That would be a problem for a fast moving bike."

"Didn't see it and ran over it. Was lookin' at the squirrel the whole time. Hadn't shot one yet today. Done kilt these three the other day."

With his hand, the boy flipped individually each of the three squirrel tails that had been tied to his handlebars with thin white string. He smiled wide when he did it.

"What's your name?" I said.

"My name's Ty, but don't call me Ty. I don't like to be called Ty. Call me Skeeter. I like Skeeter. Pa Pa gave me that name when I used to sit on his knee. I wasn't any bigger than a fart. That's what he said, not me."

"Skeeter what? What's your last name?"

"Skeeter Little. That's my name. Not Ty Little. Not Little Skeeter. Just plain Skeeter. Whatta they call you?"

"John Maynard. I work for the *Albany Chronicle*."

"You the one throwin' papers 'round here?"

"No, I write the stories that people read."

"I don't like readin'. Don't like school."

"Where you live, Skeeter?"

"There. Over yonder."

Skeeter pointed to a modest redbrick home with tan trim across Palmyra Road. There was a gray Ford pickup in the driveway parked next to a johnboat his pa pa might've used to pull gators out of the creek and river.

"Okay, Skeeter, if you're sure you're not hurt, I'm taking off now. Got a little work I need to do."

"Nah, I ain't hurt. I bleed like that 'bout every day during the summer. I've wrecked many times. John Wayne, 'member?"

"Yeah, I heard you. You ride and shoot like John Wayne. Be careful though. Watch out for those bottles. And bad guys."

"Thanks for stoppin', John Maynard. They's some mean folks that come down here. You ain't one of 'em."

"What do you mean by that?"

"Mean, there's just some mean folks 'round here."

"Skeeter, can I ask you a question?"

"I reckon you can. Question won't hurt me. The answer might."

"Are you the boy who found the girl? Were you the first one to see the body around here?"

"Yep, I believe I was. I didn't look at her the whole way. I saw her legs and went home and told Mama. I was huntin' that morning. Like I always do. Only saw her legs. Stopped lookin' after that. Didn't want to see no more."

"I'm sorry you had to go through that," I said. "I had to write a story about her. It's my job. I didn't like it, but I did it. I'll write another one when the police catch whoever did this to her."

"Like I said, mean folks come down this road. Still comin'."

"What do you mean?"

"They 'bout ran over me a couple times. Happened again this morning."

"What happened?"

"Just ridin' my bike on the side. Big van almost hit me."

"Van?"

"Yep, sure was."

"What color?" I said.

"Just like those needles on that big pine over yonder."

"Green?"

"Yep, sure was."

I got lost in thought for a few moments thinking about the green van, Big Foot, the senator, and Pearl. I was still thinking when Skeeter asked a question.

"You like fishin', John Maynard?"

"Yeah, I do. Haven't gone in a while. Used to go a lot when I was your age."

"Come back sometime, and I'll take you to the creek. I know a couple of good spots. Big bream. Big catfish. Man, they good to eat."

"I think I will. I appreciate the offer. You sure the van was green?"

"You sure you talkin' to me right now?"

CHAPTER 12

The boy, Skeeter, became visible in my rearview mirror as I drove away from the place where he had wrecked his bike after using both hands to aim a pellet gun at a squirrel. A big squirrel, he said.

I saw him racing along the dirt road with his pellet gun pressed against his shoulder and his head motionless as he rode. He could have been a Lakota warrior on horseback. Then he passed the same spot where he had seen only her legs. Two seconds later, he was out of my sight.

I returned to Uncle Jim's Lane to look for anything to indicate that the freshman senator from Georgia was acting in a way he shouldn't. Maybe there was nothing here. No story at all. Just two men, Big Foot and J.B., sharing some innocent friendship. And maybe I'd go back to see Skeeter sometime soon and he would take me fishing, I thought. At least something would come out of this.

I grew up in Albany not far from his neighborhood, and I did a lot of fishing during the summers at a pond near a library off Whispering Pines Road. I spent the rest of my time on the baseball field next to the library. Those were fun days. I never found a dead girl in the weeds like Skeeter did.

I made the right turn off Palmyra Road onto Uncle Jim's Lane where I had seen the two men along the creek yesterday morning. I could see no other cars in front of me or behind me. I looked to my left at a sweep of land covered by tall pines and live oaks hung with Spanish moss, and then to the houses and trailers along the creek-side on my right. The wind was still and the air soon-to-be-hot.

The creek ran brown, like coffee with heavy cream, and slow-moving. It had been about a month since any significant rain. The land was dry.

"Only the gnats are alive. The heat done kilt everything else." I heard a fisherman on the creek say last July.

A hundred yards from the trailer where Pearl threatened to whip my ass and feed me to the gators, something got my attention. A white Blazer was backing out of the driveway. It looked to be the same one I had seen Big Foot and the senator in.

The driver appeared to be alone and a man, but I couldn't tell for certain. He pulled out of the driveway and headed away from me and toward the section of the road that dead-ends.

I pulled over to the side of the road and thought about what Pearl said he'd do to me if I again came around the creek asking questions. I was always after a good story, but if the sacrifice was being eaten whole by a twelve-foot gator, well, I could always find something else to write about. Screw it, I decided to stay.

I figured the Blazer would drive to the dead end, turn around and come back my way. Or it would stop at one of the several houses or trailers along the way. There was only one way out of Uncle Jim's Lane. That's what I believed anyway.

I kept a sharp view along both sides of the road to avoid another Pearl surprise. I couldn't stand the thought of smelling his liquor breath one more time. If the South had used it as a weapon during the Civil War, they might've won. I was parked on the right side of the road, but I kept my car running.

Three minutes went by. Then two more. Still no Blazer. Maybe it had stopped to visit a neighbor. People living along the Kinchafoonee Creek and Flint River knew each other well. They fished and drank together and told stories at night around campfires at the water's edge. I had been a part of those evenings several times. I waited a couple more minutes and still no Blazer. I decided to move.

I drove toward the dead end and passed the last trailer on my right. The land gave way to thick piney woods on both sides of the road. Maybe the Blazer had disappeared or been driven into the creek and submerged under the mysterious water. Where the hell was it? Just like the last time, I thought. I can't find the Blazer.

I began to make the slow turn at the end of Uncle Jim's Lane and head back to the newsroom. I noticed something I hadn't seen before. About seventy-five feet into the woods were two iron posts. They were on opposite sides of a dirt road barely wide enough for one vehicle. Attached to the posts was a thick chain that swung across the road, the kind strong enough to pull a car behind a truck.

The chain looked to be padlocked. There were white signs on both posts, probably two feet long and one foot wide. The signs read: "NO TRESPASSING! PRIVATE PROPERTY."

I drove to the chain and stopped. I could see tire tracks through the dirt on the other side of the chain. Maybe that's where the Blazer went, I thought. As I had suspected, the chain was padlocked over the middle of the road. The thick and silver padlock looked new.

I stayed in my car and kept it running as I looked beyond the chain and saw that for about fifty yards the dirt road ran straight before making a gradual turn to the right, toward the creek, and then it was out of sight. I saw no other roads intersecting with the main one.

The deep thickness of the trees on both sides of the road did not surprise me. This was typical South Georgia landscape untouched by bulldozers and home building. There were many acres of green pines, oak, and cedar beyond the No Trespassing signs. The woods were dark in some places, while the morning sun was clear and warm.

I backed out of the dirt road that the Blazer could've gone down and headed back the other way. I looked at the houses and trailers along the way, and by the time I had gotten all the way to the other end of Uncle Jim's Lane, I still did not see the Blazer. I turned onto Palmyra Road.

I needed to talk with Skeeter one more time.

CHAPTER 13

I wanted to find out what was beyond the thick, silver chain and if the white Blazer had been driven down the dirt road that ran through trees, thick with vines and gray Spanish moss, and toward the creek.

If the senator was just sun bathing, drinking beer, and swimming in the Blue Hole, I would have nothing to write about. Even big-time politicians should be able to have some fun like the common man. I had to be certain that was all it was. I knew one person who might be able to help me.

Driving back toward Albany, I stopped at the same place I had earlier that morning after I had seen Skeeter lying on the ground. I parked and walked about fifty yards until I passed the spot where the Palmyra Girl had been found by the boy.

I looked on both sides of the road and into the woods for the boy. I didn't see Skeeter and headed back to my car. Then I heard him.

"Hey, you want this un? He's a big un. Gonna make good gravy. Here, he's yours if you want 'im. I can always get more."

I turned to my left and from behind a big live oak, maybe twenty-five yards away, came Skeeter on his bike. He was good at riding through tall grass and thorny underbrush. He rode straight to me and stopped.

Two feet from my face, he held up one of the biggest squirrels I had ever seen. Skeeter had the dead animal by its tail and three drops of blood from its head fell to the sand a few inches from my shoes.

"Here, I said you can have 'im," Skeeter said. "I can always shoot another one for Pa Pa."

"No, thanks, Skeeter. Probably best to go ahead and give him to your pa pa."

"Suit yourself. He'd sure taste good if you cook 'im in a big, black skillet, like Pa Pa does. Like I said, the gravy's good too."

"I'm sure you're right, Skeeter."

"Hey, why you back here?"

Skeeter took a three-foot piece of white string from his back pocket and tied one end of it to the squirrel's tail and tied the other to his handlebars. A few more drops of blood fell from its head before the bleeding stopped.

The eyes of the squirrel were wide open, and the color of its fur was a brown-gray blend that reminded me of the Kinchafoonee Creek. It was a beautiful animal in death. It only took Skeeter a few seconds to secure the squirrel to his handlebars. It looked to be something he had done many times before. He was good at it.

"Got a question for you, Skeeter."

"Dang it, that's all you do, ain't it?"

"No, sometimes I write down the answers. Then I write whole stories. I got one question, and I'm not writing down the answer."

"Well, what is it?"

"Could you take me fishing up the creek today?"

"Yep, ain't that what I said. I ain't takin' that back. I don't take back what I say."

"Yeah, you said that earlier, I just want to be sure. What about going today? Can we go now?"

"Yeah, I reckon I could take you. Pa Pa will need some bream to go with this here squirrel."

"I'd really would appreciate a fishing trip, Skeeter. Hadn't been on one for a while."

"Well, dang it, okay."

Skeeter told me his pa pa had a friend who lived on Uncle Jim's Lane, and the friend had a small johnboat that Skeeter had access to. Skeeter's parents allowed him to use the boat by himself, he said. I wasn't surprised. He may have been eleven or twelve, but he carried himself like a cocky eighteen year old.

"Follow me to my house and I'll tell my mama and then we'll go," Skeeter said.

"I'll be right behind you."

I waited in Skeeter's white-gravel driveway as he parked his bike under the carport and carried his squirrel inside. He came back a few seconds later with a plastic jug of water.

"What'd she say?"

"Say? She said bring home a mess and she'd clean 'em."

"Did you tell her you were taking me?"

"Nope, she don't ask a lot of questions. She ain't like you. I didn't say a word 'bout you. She don't like me goin' off with people she don't know. But you don't look crazy to me."

"What about the squirrel?"

"See, there you go again askin' questions. You sure you ain't a school teacher?"

"Positive. I'm a reporter. Sorry, Skeeter. I'll try not to ask too many more."

"Pa Pa's in there, he'll clean the squirrel. Said he'd help mama clean the fish. I got a baby brother and baby sister in there. They'll watch Pa Pa clean the squirrel. My daddy works at Miller Brewery. He makes beer. He don't drink it. Drinks nothing but ice tea. Sometimes a little brown liquor. Is that enough answers?"

"Just curious about bringing a dead squirrel into your house."

"Can we just go fishin' now?"

For the third time in two days I was back on Uncle Jim's Lane, and this time I stopped at the second house along the creek, as instructed by Skeeter. It was a small, brown cabin with a well-manicured yard and plenty of flowers, yellow and red roses. In the driveway was a tan Dodge Dart, one like my father used to have. Probably a '66 or '67.

I had a change of clothes in the backseat of my car that I was planning to use after work for a softball game. I played on a team called Naked Dog Walkin' with some friends. We were all decent ball players but better beer drinkers, which is what we did at Jim's Oyster Bar after our games. As Skeeter walked to the creek, I slipped into a pair of shorts, jersey, a cap and ball shoes. Much better for fishing.

The small johnboat had three seats, a twenty-five horse power Evinrude outboard motor, and a few long cane poles rigged and ready to fish with. There was a small wire basket full of crickets. The crickets were chirping in full as if they were excited to see us.

"We can use the man's bait," Skeeter said. "Pa Pa said it was okay. He done called him on the phone. We're ready."

Skeeter got into the boat with the jug of water and told me to get in the back of the boat. He started the motor and we were off, making a slow wake upstream toward were I had lost sight of the Blazer.

The air felt good on my face. I had a few more questions for Skeeter. I knew he didn't like a lot of questions, but I was going to ask anyway.

"Do you know who owns that land at the end of Uncle Jim's Lane? The place that's chained and padlocked. Do you know what I'm talking about?"

"Nope. I've seen what you're talkin' 'bout. Almost went back there to hunt. Had my twenty-two with me. Don't know who owns it."

"What stopped you?"

"Pa Pa. He said there's some folks back there you don't need to pester. Said stay away from there. So I didn't go. Never been back."

"Who owns the land? Did he say?"

"Nah, never did. I never asked."

After about a ten-minute ride, Skeeter eased over to the right bank near a cluster of tall cypress trees. We came to a shady spot, and Skeeter took a rope that was tied to the side of the boat and tied it to one of the trees. He didn't ask for my help and didn't need it. The boat remained balanced and true.

Skeeter picked up one of the cane poles and handed it to me. Then he took one himself. Both had nice rigs with bright red and white plastic bobbers. And then he passed me the crickets.

"I reckon you know how to put a cricket on a hook," Skeeter said. "Ain't but one way. Stick it in his underbelly."

"Did it before you were born," I said.

He liked what I said about baiting a hook, and he turned to me and smiled in full. First time I'd seen that out of him. It was a good-looking smile.

"This here spot is where the red-bellies bed in the spring," Skeeter said. "Beddin' season is over, but we can still catch a few. Won't be as many. They love the cypress trees. Purty, ain't they?"

"I love them, too, Skeeter."

We fished under the shade of the cypress trees for about twenty minutes and each of us caught four nice red-bellies, all between seven and ten inches. Skeeter put them in his fish basket he had tied to the side of the boat. A few minutes after I caught my last fish, I heard water splashing from the other side of the creek. I thought first of big alligators.

I turned and looked in the direction of the splashing. It was coming about seventy-five yards downstream where I could see a group of people swimming along a brown-sandy beach. I counted five girls wearing shorts and T-shirts.

They all looked to be teenagers or a little older. A couple of them had black hair and they all looked well-tanned. There were no boats or canoes nearby indicating how they might have gotten to that beach. I didn't see any men or boys with them.

I asked Skeeter if we could stop fishing and if he could give me a boat ride downstream. I wanted to see if there was anyone else with the girls, but I didn't tell Skeeter that.

"Yeah, I reckon. We got enough fish to go with the squirrel. They some big gators 'round here. They may jump in the boat and get us."

"Yeah, I've heard that same thing from other folks. It's never happened to me before. I been on this creek several times since I was your age."

We put our cane poles in the bottom of the boat, and Skeeter guided the boat downstream, staying in the middle of the creek. When we got to where the girls were swimming, I asked him if he knew who they were.

"Nah, never seen 'em before. Ain't got time for no girls. They don't like fishin' and killin' squirrels."

"You're right, Skeeter. They're hard to understand sometimes. But I reckon we are, too."

With a closer look at the girls in the water, my guess concerning their ages seemed about right.

"Skeeter, how do you think those girls got to that beach?" I said. "I don't see a boat anywhere. Do you?"

"There you go with those questions again. I ain't in school now. It's summer, you know. You sound like my teacher more and more. "

"Is there anything back on that property?" I said. "A cabin? A trailer? Maybe a house? Do you know of anything?"

"I thought we were fishin' and here you are again with your questions. I don't know what's back there. Maybe nothin' but trees and squirrels and deer and monsters and ghosts. Dang, I don't know."

We passed the girls on the beach and after fifty yards or so, I asked Skeeter to turn around and drive by them again.

"I thought this was a fishin' trip," Skeeter said. "Not a beach party."

As he made a slow, wide turn in the middle of the creek, I saw two big gators sunning themselves on the bank opposite from where the girls were swimming. They looked immovable and metallic. Ground-level gray tanks on four legs. Skeeter saw them too.

"Looky there, newspaper man," Skeeter said. "See, they big as this here boat, ain't they?"

"Maybe bigger."

We passed the girls for the second time, this time a bit closer, and I noticed somebody had joined them along the sandy beach. Standing near the water and with all the girls in front of him was Pearl. He saw me the same time I saw him.

As soon as he saw us ease by, he extended his right arm to the blue sky and waved to me with his middle finger only. I waved back with my right hand but had all my fingers extended together. He looked pissed. I bet his breath still smells like liquor, I thought.

"You know 'im?" Skeeter said.

"We've met briefly. We're not friends, if that's what you mean. He'll never invite me over for a fish fry."

"That's the one Pa Pa told me 'bout. Said to stay away from him. Pearl is what they call 'im. That's the only name I ever heard."

"That's what I heard, too."

"What's he doin' with 'em girls, you reckon?" Skeeter said.

"Watching them swim, it looks like."

As we passed the beach where Pearl and the five girls were, I turned to look at them one more time.

All of the girls were now out of the water and walking single file into the woods. Pearl was behind the fifth girl, and I could see something sticking out of the back of his jeans. It looked to be a gun with large white-pearl handle.

CHAPTER 14

I dropped Skeeter at his house and went home and changed into my work clothes, before returning to the newsroom. Driving toward downtown Albany, I decided I had to find a way onto the property where the girls and Pearl had disappeared into the woods.

I needed to know what was back there besides squirrels and deer and monsters and ghosts.

I became more convinced that there was something happening on the Kinchafoonee that required the full attention of my newspaper. Five teenage girls being ushered from a sandy beach by Pearl with a gun was enough for me. I had to know more. I had to tell Mickey about this.

This time along the creek I hadn't seen Big Foot or Senator Whitfield, but I wondered if they had ever visited the property that was chained and padlocked. The property where the girls were. And I wondered who owned it. Did it belong to Pearl? That should be easy to find out, I thought. I decided to make a visit to the Dougherty County Courthouse before going to the newsroom.

I parked along Pine Avenue in front of the newsroom but walked in another direction with the sun now high and hot. I thought about Skeeter and smiled. He was a piece of work. Maybe we'd take another boat ride and fish again together. I had no interest in shooting squirrels from his bicycle.

What I was interested in now was inside the courthouse.

The young girls I saw on the creek had me thinking about the dead one I had just written about. My first stop was downstairs to the APD and Detective Vince McGill's office for any additional information about the story. Maybe the cops were getting closer to an arrest.

McGill was standing next to a red Coke machine talking to a couple of uniformed lawmen when I entered the complex. He saw me come in and motioned to the empty chair in front of his desk. I took a seat there and in just a couple of minutes he approached me. We shook hands, and he sat in the chair behind his desk and I sat down in front of it. He was wearing a dark blue tie, still tied in full, and a pressed white shirt.

"So you must've already heard?" McGill said.

"Heard what?"

"Well, by that response, I guess you haven't. I was planning to call you sometime this afternoon."

"Here I am. What do you got?"

"We got some information on the girl," McGill said. "The one we found off Palmyra Road. The young girl."

He opened a brown folder on top of his desk, put on black reading glasses, and leaned over the folder. I took my notepad and pen from my back pocket as he began to talk slowly, as he had done the morning her body was found. He was considerate of my note taking.

McGill said the APD had identified the girl, and she had been living with her uncle in Mitchell County, just south of Albany. The girl and her uncle were both born in Nicaragua and had arrived in the United States about three months ago. They had fled Nicaragua after the girl's parents, two sisters, and a brother were all killed by the Contras as the civil war in that country continued.

She was drawing water from a well when a mortar hit her home, killing her family. The Contras were financed by the U.S. government in efforts to topple the Nicaraguan government. McGill didn't tell me that. I already knew it.

The two had been given refugee status by the time they arrived in Miami but later came to South Georgia seeking work in the vegetable fields with others from the war in Central America, McGill said. He stopped and looked at me. I repeated to him what he had told me. My notes, so far, were good.

"What's her name?" I said.

"Maria Rios. She was three months away from her sixteenth birthday. She was the oldest child in her family. Always took care of her sisters and her brother, the uncle said. She was a great kid."

"And her uncle?"

"Gabriel Rios. He's thirty-eight. His brother was Maria's father. Gabriel lost his wife and two children in the war. Hell of thing, Maynard."

"How did you contact the uncle?"

"He found us through the Mitchell County Sheriff's Office. Told them the girl was missing and then the Mitchell County boys called us. We got the call around nine this morning. They brought the uncle to us to identify the body. He was carrying a rosary and made the sign of the cross over his niece. And prayed and prayed. It was an awful thing to see that man collapse like he did over her body. Everybody in his family is dead."

Gabriel told lawmen the day before her body was found, Maria had been working in the Mitchell County fields alongside her uncle and several others from Nicaragua. Around three that afternoon she stopped to take a break. She walked to the edge of the field, part of five thousand acres owned by C. W. "Possum" Walker, where portable toilets had been placed. She never returned from her bathroom break, McGill said.

"Why did you just get a call today? That was three days ago. My story ran two days ago."

"I don't have a good answer for you, Maynard. Other than the Mitchell County boys can be mighty slow. Don't print that."

"I won't."

"We're still working on this case, and we're probably going to need their help down there."

"Any leads on who did it?"

"No, not yet. Just a damn shame. We'll find who did it. The GBI is on it, and we've got area law enforcement involved. We'll find 'em."

"Anything else I need to know? Anything you want to tell the public?"

"Just the usual," McGill said. "The investigation is continuing. We'll find who did it."

"I'll have something in tomorrow's paper. Thanks, Detective McGill."

"Thank you for keeping the public aware of this case."

McGill had given me enough information for a follow-up Mickey could run in tomorrow's paper. I left his office but had one more stop to make in the courthouse before returning to the newsroom. I opened the door to the Dougherty County Tax Assessor's Office and there she was.

Betty Jane Futch had worked for the county government for forty-two years and the past eighteen she had been in charge of the tax assessor's office. I had gotten information from her three or four times since I started working for the *Chronicle* a few years earlier. Always professional. Always exact.

No one, dead or alive, knew more about the workings of the county government than Mrs. Futch. Dust never gathered in a closet without first conferring with her.

She was almost five ten but weighed barely enough to keep a light wind from swaying her when she walked down Pine Avenue on her way to work each morning. She lived with her husband four blocks away on Jefferson Avenue. Never in eighteen years in the tax assessor's office had she taken sick leave. Probably never been sick in her life.

Her dresses were always pressed but never pretentious. She wore her gray hair with bangs half way down her forehead. Every hair, every day, always in place. She wore little makeup and was attractive without it. If you needed accurate information, she was the one.

When I walked into her office, she had her back to me as she was returning a large book to the shelves. She spoke before I did while still facing the books on the shelves.

"Well, Mr. Maynard, I haven't seen you in a while," Mrs. Futch said. "What can I do for you today? What are you looking for?"

"How'd you know it was me, Mrs. Futch?"

"Never mind that, Mr. Maynard. It's not how you know things, it's what you do with the things you know."

"Good point, Mrs. Futch. I'll remember that."

Now she turned to face me and walked to where I was standing.

"I hope you remember it," she said. "It's something my daddy told me long ago."

"Sounds like a wise man."

"He was. Now, there's a reason you came to see me today. What is it?"

I told Mrs. Futch I wanted to know who owned the property along the Kinchafoonee at the end of Uncle Jim's Lane. The same place I had seen Pearl and the five young girls in the creek. She didn't ask why I wanted to know. She never asked anyone that question who was researching public documents in her office.

"Can you tell me which one of those big books will tell me what I need to know?" I said. "Who owns that property?"

"No, Mr. Maynard, I will not," she said. "Since you are my only tax-paying citizen in here right now, you'll get my full attention."

She moved from one shelf to another, then another and found the book she was looking for and placed it on a long wooden table in the middle of the room. The book's cover was faded brown with a crinkled black spine.

She opened it to the Table of Contents and ran her right index finger down to the middle of the page. She did all of this in a precise way as if it was a scientific experiment.

I stood quiet and motionless a few feet from her and the book. She turned several pages and stopped at page seventy-nine. She turned five more pages and stopped again. She leaned over the page for a few moments. I said nothing the whole time.

"Here it is," she said. "This is what you are looking for. This is the deed for the property you asked about, Mr. Maynard."

Mrs. Futch left the big book and returned to her desk and the papers she was filing in a metal cabinet.

"If you have any questions, Mr. Maynard, don't hesitate to ask."

"Yes, I know. Thank you Mrs. Futch. You are always helpful and I appreciate that."

I took my notepad and pen and began to read and take notes from the deed. The one hundred thirty-five acres of land included about a quarter of a mile along the bank of the creek. The beach where I saw the girls and Pearl, I thought.

The land belonged to Myrtle Jean Shellhouse from Mitchell County. I wrote down the name with a question mark next to it.

I noticed that Mrs. Futch had made a telephone call and was speaking with someone, but I couldn't hear the nature of the conversation. I looked at the deed and the name a final time before closing the big book and returning it to its proper place on the shelf.

Mrs. Futch had finished her phone conversation and answered my question before I asked it.

"That was Darlene from downstairs," she said. "She handles building permits and said there's no record of the county issuing one on that piece of property you asked about. Nothing on our books."

"Okay, thank you Mrs. Futch. That was the answer to my first question. What else am I going to ask you?"

"Myrtle Jean Shellhouse is married to C. W. Walker. He's the chairman of the Mitchell County Commission. They been married probably forty years. Her granddaddy bought that piece of land on the creek not long after the war of Yankee Conquest. She got it because the Shellhouse family didn't produce any boys. Myrtle Jean had two sisters but both died when they were teenagers. Malaria, I believe. We don't have that problem around here anymore. Myrtle was the youngest of the three."

"Mrs. Futch, can I ask you a question?"

"I thought you just did."

"Is there anything about people and property around here that you don't know?"

"No, Mr. Maynard, I don't believe so."

Before I thanked Mrs. Futch for her help and left the deed office for the newsroom, I realized something about the names I had just heard and written.

Myrtle Jean's husband, C. W. "Possum" Walker, owned the land where Maria Rios worked and was last seen alive there.

"What do you know about C. W. Walker, Mrs. Futch?" I said.

"He's like a lot of them around here. Commissioners that is. He talks a lot but doesn't say anything. He inherited some land and money too. Thinks he's smarter than everybody because of that. I don't want to see my name in your paper saying *that*, Mr. Maynard."

"You won't, Mrs. Futch. I just wanted a little background from you. I don't know the things you know. And you know I'm never going to quote you."

"He really talks big now. C. W. that is."

"Why is that?"

"His nephew is our U.S. Senator Jefferson Beauregard Whitfield. Lovely name, don't you think, Mr. Maynard?"

"You sure about that, Mrs. Futch?"

"You just asked me if there was anything about people and property I didn't know. Remember? The answer's still no."

"Yes, I remember. Thank you so much for your help. I've got to get to the newsroom and write a story."

"For tomorrow's paper?"

"Yes ma'am."

"Well, good luck, and it was good seeing you again. My pleasure to help you."

"Thanks again."

I left the courthouse for the newsroom where I wrote a follow-up story based on the new information Detective McGill had given me on Maria Rios and her uncle. The information I had learned from Mrs. Futch I typed up and placed in a folder in my desk.

Now I knew who the girl was but not who had done those terrible things to her.

CHAPTER 15

I invited Abby for dinner at my house on a Friday few days after my follow-up story. We were not scheduled to work the next day and I had a plan for us. Just the two of us.

I grilled chicken, Abby made a salad and prepared two baked potatoes heavy with sour cream and oven-baked rolls. I popped the cork off a bottle of Chardonnay. The wine went down easy.

After dinner, we talked while sitting on the sofa. I played an Allman Brothers' record, *Eat a Peach*. Abby's favorite song on it was "Blue Sky:" *Walk along the river, sweet lullaby, it just keeps on flowing/ It don't worry 'bout where it's going, no, no/ Don't fly mister blue bird, I'm just walking down the road/ Early morning sunshine, tell me all I need to know...*

I had the music low because I wanted to share my Saturday plan with her. I had already told her about Skeeter taking me fishing and seeing Pearl and the young girls along the creek.

"I want you to do something fun with me tomorrow," I said. "I got a plan for us. It's going to be fun."

"Do we have to wait until tomorrow to have some fun? Can't you have fun anytime you want, Johnny Boy? I don't like putting important things off. I woman wants certain things. You know what I mean?"

She moved closer to me and put her arm around my neck. She kissed me on the mouth. It took us a few moments to finish. I almost forgot what I needed to say.

"Well, I declare Miss Abby, my, my, my. You are the Belle of the South and such salty language from a lady like yourself. What is this world comin' to?"

"Are you trying to be Rhett Butler or Richard Pryor?"

"Oh, that's funny, Abby. I'm Rhett Butler and you're Scarlett O'Hara."

"John, I'd rather for us to be Bonnie and Clyde. You know how I feel about patriarchy. About the great myth of the Old South."

"I'm just having some fun. Bonnie and Clyde. Now that's good, Abby. That's funny. You should be laughing. You're my funny girl tonight."

"Tonight will take care of itself, Johnny Boy. What kind of plans to you have for us tomorrow? I want to hear them."

I told Abby I wanted to take her to float on inner tubes on the Kinchafoonee Creek. We had done that together in the past and enjoyed it. This would give me another opportunity to look at the beach where I saw Pearl and the five girls the day Skeeter took me fishing.

That scene on the beach still had me thinking that something was happening in those woods that shouldn't be. I needed another full look at that part of the creek.

"John, if you think something is happening up there that's against the law, then why don't you go to the police? Just go tell the cops what you think."

"What I think? That's not enough to convince the cops to go out there and ask questions. That's not enough for them to go on. You know that."

"So why are we going?"

"Like I said, to have some fun. Float down the creek. Swim in the Blue Hole. Drink a cold beer together on a hot day. Lots of reasons. Maybe fool around. Who knows?"

"Okay, all of that sounds like fun."

"That's right," I said. "And I just want one more look at that beach. That's all. Maybe there's nothing going on up there in the woods. Maybe nothing at all."

"You're just going to look, right?"

"That's all. Just take a look. We'll have a great day on the creek. I promise."

"Well, it does sound like a fun day."

"Good. We're a team, aren't we?"

"Just don't ever call me Scarlett again."

"I thought I was funny."

"No, I'll tell you when you're funny. But we are a team, Johnny Boy."

I rolled over Abby gently about eight-thirty the next morning as she was sleeping. My bedroom clock was on the nightstand on her side of the bed. She was naked under the sheet. I didn't mind at all having to cross the bed to see the clock. Her eyes remained closed. Her dark hair covering most of the white pillow slip.

She looked perfect in sleep. All the touches, good kisses, and love-making was just what I wanted. And needed. The way she was with me made me think everything we did was good for her, too. She looked happy in sleep.

I got up and made coffee, scrambled eggs, and toast. A few minutes later she came into the kitchen wearing a red T-shirt that belonged to me. She sat down at the table as I poured her a cup of coffee. She added cream and sugar. Two cubes of sugar always.

"Good morning, Miss Scar...," I said. "I forgot. Those days are over. Right?"

"Too early for your jokes, Johnny Boy. Way too early."

After breakfast, I read the paper and Abby read a few pages from *To Kill a Mockingbird*. She had already read the book three times.

Later in the morning I tied two large black inner tubes to the top of my car while Abby made sandwiches and packed a white and red Budweiser Styrofoam cooler with water and beer and food. Around eleven we both got into our cars and headed toward the Kinchafoonee Creek. The forecast called for ninety-seven degrees. Humidity would be almost as high. Perfect weather for gnats and rattlesnakes. And for staying in the water with the woman you love.

Abby parked her blue Plymouth Duster at a public access road along the creek a few miles from Uncle Jim's Lane. She got in the car with me, and we drove a few minutes upstream and parked at another public access spot. From there, the float was about three miles by water to Abby's car.

How long it took depended on how much time and how many beers might be consumed at the Blue Hole and other places along the creek. Floaters could make a day of it.

We parked and I put the inner tubes in the water and tied the ice chest to mine. We took off slowly downstream in the brown water.

Abby wore a blue bikini and a straw hat with a yellow cloth band around it. Her face was shaded from the sun. She had a gorgeous tan from our afternoons together at Panama City Beach and along the creek and the Flint River.

We held hands the first hundred yards or so with our inner tubes pressed against the other. The water was warm and the sun was rising.

"John, you've never actually seen gators on the creek, have you?"

"Well, no, not *on* the creek."

"What does that mean?"

"Oh, Abby, there you go again concerned with *meaning*. I've told you many times, it's all about experience. To hell with meaning. Here's the only question you are not allowed to ask: What is the meaning of life? I know how you reporters like to ask questions."

"That's right. I forgot. You are my great philosopher. The Almighty Wise One. Experience over meaning every time. So says the Great One. I'm honored to be in your presence, Almighty One."

"And don't you ever forget it."

We had been on the creek several times together and had never seen a gator. She didn't need to know about the two I had seen when Skeeter took me fishing. A wise philosopher could keep a secret.

We floated and talked for the next thirty minutes until we came to the Blue Hole. This was an underground spring that fed cold and clear water into the creek. We swam there for several minutes. Then we rested and had sandwiches and beers. This was a popular spot on the creek, but that day it was all ours. We got back on our inner tubes and headed downstream.

Soon we were near the spot along the creek where I had fished with Skeeter. I could also see the empty beach where I had seen Pearl and the girls. I pointed it out to Abby.

"There's the spot. That's where I saw them. Right there on that stretch of beach."

"Your new best friend, right?"

"Yeah, we're close all right. Tight you might say. Me and Pearl."

I grabbed the rope connected to Abby's inner tube and was able to guide us to the beach. I could see no other people on the creek.

"John, we probably don't need to stay here. Let's go somewhere else."

"We're not staying. I'm just going to walk up the little hill and through the trees. You stay here. I'll be right back."

"Nope."

"Nope what?"

"I'm going too," Abby said. "We'll take a quick look and come right back."

"Okay, let's go together then."

CHAPTER 16

We held hands walking on the beach then up a sandy hill along an eighteen-inch wide footpath that led into thick trees and underbrush. Blackberry bushes ready for picking lined the trail. The sweet aroma of honeysuckle was everywhere.

We were shoeless and mindful of water moccasins. About fifty yards from the creek, I saw it. I didn't know what I was looking for until I saw it. But there it was.

The long wooden building was one floor and painted fresh green. It reminded me of a military barracks. Or a place teenagers might stay for a summer camp. It was about a hundred- feet long. I didn't see anybody or any vehicles near it.

A dirt road led to the building and probably the same one I saw at the end of Uncle Jim's Lane, I thought. The road that was posted, chained, and padlocked. We kept walking toward the building to get a better look. Abby stopped me when we were about thirty feet from it.

"All right, John, we've seen whatever this is. Let's go back to the creek. I don't like being here."

We heard it before I was able to respond to her. There was a vehicle coming down the road toward us and the long building. It was moving fast and getting close. If we returned to the creek, there was a chance we would be seen. We needed a quick decision.

I saw a green shed that could've been used to store tools and yard equipment. I led Abby to the shed and out of sight. We weren't far from the parking area in front of the building.

"John, what are we doing!"

"We don't have a choice now. We might be seen. Let's get behind here and stay quiet. We'll get back to the creek in a minute. "

"I know we should've kept going. I knew it. There's no reason for us to be here, John."

"Okay, okay. I get it. I screwed up. Let's stop talking for now."

The vehicle was getting closer. We were out of view behind the shed. That's where we waited. I looked out from the corner of the shed closest to the driveway and could identify the approaching vehicle. It looked to be the same white Blazer that I followed from the Monkey Palace the morning Abby took me there to get my car. Senator Jefferson Beauregard Whitfield and Big Foot were in the vehicle that day.

I saw the Blazer stop near the front door of the long building before I secured myself completely behind the shed with Abby. I could no longer see what was happening but I could hear it all. Two doors opened and shut.

Then I sensed something was moving on the ground behind the shed with us. That's where my focus turned next.

Slithering on the ground just a couple of feet from Abby was a four-foot-long water moccasin. I could see part of its white underbelly and its gray-black body. It was twice as thick as the baseball bat I used on my college team. They could be aggressive. And they could kill you. I saw the snake before Abby did and had to act.

I reached for Abby with my left hand and pulled her to me. I placed my right hand over her mouth. I knew she would scream when she saw the snake. Her eyes grew wide when she looked to the ground and saw that I had pulled her out of the path of the snake.

She didn't scream. The snake disappeared into some honeysuckle bushes ten seconds later. Our attention refocused on whoever had gotten out of the Blazer.

We heard two voices and I recognized each one. I looked around the corner of the shed to be sure I was right. It was Big Foot and Pearl. They had set a half gallon of Jack Daniels and two red plastic cups on top of the Blazer. Then I positioned myself behind the shed with Abby where I could no longer see the two men, but we could hear what they were saying.

Abby was looking at the ground for other snakes. We were not in a good situation and could do nothing but wait. Now I wished I had listened to Abby and stayed on the creek. Then I heard the whiskey being poured into the cups.

"We need a toast, don't you think, Big Foot?" Pearl said.

"Sure do. I got somethin' to go with it. Done rolled a fat one. Goes good with Black Jack. The shit will get you fucked up in a hurry. It's my latest shipment."

There wasn't any talking for a few moments as they drank and smoked with the smell of marijuana now engulfing the area. I stood next to Abby with my hands on her shoulders. Damn, I wish they'd go inside so we could get the hell out of here, I thought.

"That's some good one-hit-shit," Pearl said. "Just like that weed we had down in Honduras. That shit made you see Jesus."

"Pearl, I thought you were Jesus?"

"I reckon I could be."

"Let's toast to Jesus," Big Foot said.

I could hear the whiskey being poured again as their voices were silent. The smell of the joint still floated above the shed. They began to talk again a few moments later.

"When's the next group comin'?" Big Foot said.

"Said they'd be here 'round nine. Got some more purty ones."

"I'll tell the boys. Got some new customers comin' out."

"What about your friend J.B.?" Pearl said. "The senator. He seems to like it out here."

"My friend? He's your friend too. You knew him before I did."

"Yeah, I reckon I did. He served his country down in Honduras. Just like I did. He knows 'bout the new shipment tonight. Don't know if he's comin' or not."

"So you met him down there, right? In Honduras? Isn't that what you told me?"

"Yep. Fightin' the commies, by God, in Nicaragua. Ain't America great? He was real busy down there. Got along with everybody, especially the young people."

"He sure is a good customer," Big Foot said.

"Yep, reckon so."

The next thing we heard was one of the two coughing for a few moments after being overcome by the joint. Several seconds passed, then more talking.

"Damn, that shit's good," Pearl said. "I'm still Jesus."

"Well, Jesus, I got a question for you."

"Yes, my son."

"Did you take care of that problem you told me about?"

"Oh, yeah. That ain't a problem no more."

"How did you handle it?"

"It's under the witch tree. Ain't nobody gonna find it."

"The witch tree?" Big Foot said.

"Trust me."

"Okay, Jesus, I trust you. No reason not to."

CHAPTER 17

Time moved on the back of a dead turtle before we heard Big Foot and Pearl get into the Blazer and drive away. Later we figured only eight to ten minutes had passed when we were hiding behind the shed.

When we could no longer hear the vehicle, I leaned around the shed and saw no one. I grabbed Abby's hand, and we jogged back to the beach and to our inner tubes. We got on them and paddled off as quickly as we could.

We said nothing until at least two hundred yards of creek stretched between us and the beach that marked where the long building was.

"That was a great beach trip you took me on, John. You know how much I love relaxing at the beach. Remember our trip to Destin last month? Well, this was much more fun. Don't you think?"

"What was your favorite part? Reading poetry on the beach? Walking on the beach at sunset? Making love at midnight?"

"Oh, no, John. Not even close. My favorite part of this beach trip is when the water moccasin visited us. No question about it."

"You're funny, Abby. Just one of the many reasons why I love you so much."

"You see me laughing?"

"Maybe on the inside."

"Not even there," she said.

"Okay, that was the wrong question. I've got another one for you."

"I can't wait."

"What in the hell did we just hear back there?"

"John, I don't know what we heard back there. I was trying not to get bit by a damn snake."

"Abby, you heard the same thing I did. Tell me what you think."

"I don't know what's happening back there, but I bet it's something that shouldn't be."

"Shipment? Customers? Witch tree? What does it mean, Abby?"

"Drugs maybe. Probably drugs. What else is being shipped around here that's done so in the middle of the woods? Probably after midnight."

"Do they have drug connections in Nicaragua?" I said. "Maybe so, Abby. Maybe so."

"So Senator Whitfield of Camilla, Georgia, is involved in the Central American drug trade?"

"Maybe so," I said.

"I guess he wouldn't be the first politician to disappoint his constituents. No surprise there, John."

"Not at all," I said.

"That would explain why he's been spending time at the Monkey Palace with Big Foot. So you think they're both dealing?"

"I don't know, Abby. Maybe they're just having a pot party in the woods. A lot of that is going on around here. Not selling, just smoking the shit out of it."

"Could be but could be more than just that."

"That would explain the girls," I said.

"What girls? I didn't see any girls. I didn't hear any. Did you?"

"No, I didn't, but I did a few days ago when I was fishing with Skeeter. Don't you remember? I told you about the girls."

"Yeah, okay, I remember now. Well, if you're going to have a pot party, you need plenty of girls, right John?"

"I would think so."

A group of mallard ducks flew overhead and landed in the middle of the creek about fifty feet behind us. Their green heads and yellow bills were a sharp contrast to the brown water. They swam together to the south bank and began feeding along the water's edge. They stayed close to one another and passed a branch extending over the water. Four turtles were sitting in a row on the branch. I watched the animals for a few moments until the creek turned and they were out of sight.

We were both quiet for a few minutes. The Kincahfoonee was still slow and peaceful. We only heard sounds of birds.

"Abby?"

"What is it?"

"Did they say Nicaragua?"

"Who said what?

"You know what I'm talking about," I said. "When we were behind the shed, did Big Foot and Pearl mention Nicaragua?"

"I think so. Fighting the commies I think is what one of them said. So, what does that mean?"

"The girl, Abby. She was from Nicaragua. The one I wrote about. That was Pearl who said it. I know that voice. I've heard it up close. Even smelled it up close a couple times."

"I remember what your story said. Maria Rios had come here with her uncle. What was his name?"

"Gabriel. Her uncle is Gabriel. Her family was killed by the Contras in Nicaragua."

"So they say Nicaragua," Abby said, "and Maria Rios and her uncle were from Nicaragua. What does it mean, John? You trying to put those two together? You tell me how they fit. I'm listening."

"I don't know if they fit, Abby. It just struck me, that's all. I don't know if any of this fits at all."

"Something's happening back there. I don't know about Nicaragua but something's happening back there."

"One more question, Abby. Just one more."

"Please make this the last one. I just want to go home. This didn't turn out the way we planned."

"Okay, this is the last one. What does it mean to take care of your problem next to the witch tree? Pearl said that, too. Tell me what that means."

"First of all, I don't know what kind of problem he had, and the last time I saw a witch tree, I was watching *The Wizard of Oz* on television with my family. You keep asking me questions I don't have the answers to. I just wanted to be with you on the creek today."

"You're no help, Abby."

"I'm a pretty good reporter, Johnny Boy, but I need just a little bit more than that. I don't know what any of this means. I do want to find out who killed Maria Rios. I don't want any other girls to end up like her."

Ten minutes later our float ended where we had parked Abby's car. We loaded the inner tubes on top of her Duster and secured them with a couple of straps. We picked up my car and drove both cars away from the Kinchafoonee and back to my house. The long wooden building and the conversation we heard between Pearl and Big Foot remained a mystery for now. This wouldn't be our last trip to the creek, I thought.

We had begun to believe that whatever was happening on the creek was something we needed to know. It wasn't a pot party on the creek. We were convinced of that.

CHAPTER 18

Monday morning we decided to talk to Mickey at the newsroom, hoping he would give us some guidance on what we heard along the creek over the weekend.

He wore dark blue slacks, brown leather shoes and no socks, a white shirt with a loose-fitting red-striped tie. Standard newsroom dress for Mickey.

He was editing a story and making pencil corrections on the four pieces of paper that had been taped together. He juggled coffee and cigarettes in between the editing. He pointed to the two black vinyl chairs in front of his desk and we sat down.

Three minutes later he had finished editing. He folded the four pages and placed the story in a wire basket sitting on his desk. Then he leaned back in his big leather chair and looked at us with smoke swirling over his head like a crown on a king. Homage to the newspaper gods.

"What do you two got going this morning?" Mickey said. "What do you need?"

"Mickey, we need to share something with you," I said. "We need some direction on this story we're on."

"Go ahead," Mickey said. "Give me what you got."

I went through the story in a little more than a minute. I included the fact that the wife of C. W. "Possum" Walker, a Mitchell County commissioner, owns the land along the Kinchafoonee Creek where we saw the longhouse and overheard the conversation between Pearl and Big Foot. I left out no detail of the conversation, including the water moccasin.

I reminded Mickey what I had told him earlier about seeing Big Foot and Senator Whitfield together at the Monkey Palace and along the creek. He hadn't forgotten that part of the story.

"Jesus H. Christ!" Mickey said. "What the hell kind of goddamn story is this. Big Foot, Pearl, Sugar Baby, Skeeter, and Possum! Maynard, you and Abby work for a newspaper or are you writing children's books? *Jesus H. Christ.*"

"Mickey, we don't know what kind of story this is," Abby said. "That's just it. That's the problem. We just don't know. We don't want other girls to end up like Maria Rios."

"I thought you'd like the names," I said, "but we need to know if you want us to pursue this. We both think there's a story out there. We just got to get to it."

"You agree, Abby?" Mickey said.

"Yes, I do," she said. "There's just a lot of pieces we need to try to put together. I think there's something illegal happening on the creek. Now it could be just a bunch good 'ol boys partying and smoking pot. But it could be much more than that. We need to find out, Mickey."

"Goddamnit, do it then. For the next few days, you two work your sources on this story," Mickey said. "See whether you have a story out there. Find out either way and let me know something. If there's nothing there, then we move on to something else. Got it?"

"Okay, that sounds good," I said. "We'll start today and keep you posted on what we find."

Later that morning we drove to Mitchell County and the property owned by C. W. "Possum" Walker. There we hoped to find Gabriel Rios and interview him about his niece's disappearance and death. We searched for any connection between Maria Rios and the girls I had seen with Pearl along the creek, not far from where Maria's body was found by Skeeter.

We took U.S. Highway 19 south out of Albany toward Camilla passing large swaths of pecan orchards and fields planted with peanuts and cotton. The drive to Walker's farm would be around thirty minutes and before arriving, we passed a few vegetable stands along the highway near the little town of Baconton. Vegetables maybe picked by Maria's hands.

Abby looked out the window and was quiet for a few moments. The planted fields were lush green. New life emerging from the earth. She put her left hand on my shoulder before asking the question.

"What do you think she was like?"

"Who was like what?"

"Maria. What do you think she was like, John? Don't you think about her?"

"Yeah, I think about her."

"So? Tell me."

"She was probably beautiful like you," I said. "Probably kind like you. Probably loved her family like you. And probably loved the truth like you."

"We could've been sisters, John. That poor girl. To lose her family and then her own life. We've got our lives. We've got our families. People can be so cruel to other people. So cruel."

"It had to be unimaginable fear in the end for her," I said. "It had to be. All that pain and suffering before she died. And all that pain and suffering in her country. Her home."

"It's sickening, and we got to find out who did this to her," Abby said. "We've got to make sure it doesn't happen again. Other girls may be at risk, John."

"I agree. That's why we need to see her uncle. To see what he can tell us."

Ten minutes later we saw a large green and white sign on the right side of the road that read, "Walker's Vegetable Farm Half Mile Ahead." Then we followed the sign's arrow and turned right on a dirt road, a couple of miles before entering Camilla.

Piney forests lined both sides of the road in the beginning. A few giant live oaks towered near some of the pines. The land reminded me of the property along the Kinchafoonee where the longhouse was. I drove slowly and saw something in the road.

A long black snake was crossing the road in front of us, and I stopped to let it pass.

"Don't worry about this one," I said. "He's just a big, beautiful king snake. He won't hurt you. He may hurt that water moccasin that we saw. But he won't hurt us."

"You used the words beautiful and snake in the same sentence. I like the way you said that, John."

"Well, there's a few things I can teach you. We got to be open to beauty wherever it is. There are all kinds of beauty in this world, Abby. Don't you think?"

"I do, John. We all need more beauty in our lives."

We waited a few moments before the snake disappeared in the green underbrush. We watched the black fade into green. Then we continued to the vegetable farm in search of Gabriel Rios.

The large open vegetable fields began to appear on our right, seconds after Mr. King Snake crossed the road. We saw another sign indicating the land was owned by C. W. Walker. Back-bending workers picked many acres of land in the hot sun, filling baskets with tomatoes and peppers and cucumbers.

We turned right onto another dirt road where the farm headquarters appeared to be located. I parked in the shade of an island of tall pines. We walked to a group of workers sitting under a green pavilion and drinking from white Styrofoam cups. They were all dirty, sweaty, and wearing big-brimmed straw hats.

I asked one of the men where we could find Gabriel Rios. The man pointed to a nearby gray warehouse where vegetables were being readied for shipping. The man said Gabriel was wearing a straw hat and a blue T-shirt and that he usually drove a forklift. We thanked the man and walked about seventy-five yards to the warehouse.

The building was about as half as long as a football field. Six large fans were positioned throughout it. The fans kept warm air circulating. And blew the gnats away so they didn't harass the workers. About twenty men and women worked inside the warehouse. In the center of the building, we saw a man sitting on a yellow forklift. He wore a blue T-shirt and straw hat.

The workers appeared to be on break as we approached the man on the forklift. He rested with the engine off. "Excuse me, sir," I said. "Are you Gabriel Rios?"

He looked at us and then around the warehouse, as if I had spoken to someone else. He wore jeans and tattered black work boots. Both the front and back of his T-shirt were sweat-soaked. His dark skin was made darker by the dust and dirt that had accumulated there from the hard work he did. His eyes were deep into his face. They were the color of Abby's eyes. They were the color of Maria Rios' eyes.

Gabriel was around five ten and slender. There was hardness and strength in his chest and arms. He leaned on the steering wheel and his eyes settled on us.

"It is my name," Gabriel said. "For what reason you want to know?"

"I'm John Maynard of the *Albany Chronicle* and this is Abby Sinclair. We work together at the paper."

From my back pocket I took a notepad and a black pen. Gabriel looked at them but said nothing. I extended my hand and he shook it. Abby did the same with the same response.

"You want tomatoes?" Gabriel said. "You want peppers? They take your money over there. Alma will take your money and give you tomatoes. Best tomatoes in America. I help pick them."

Gabriel pointed to a counter near an office door where vegetables were available for sale. Three women stood behind the long counter. We looked in that direction then back at him.

"Mr. Rios, we didn't come here to buy anything," Abby said. "We'd like to ask you a couple of questions about your niece, Maria. It will just take a minute or two. We won't get in the way of your work."

"Maria?" Gabriel said. "She is with the Virgin Mary. She is with her family. My family is at the same place. I can't talk about it no more. I have no tears left. My tears are all dead. Just like my family."

"Mr. Rios, we are so sorry about what happened to Maria," Abby said, "and I can't imagine the pain you feel. No one but you understands how awful it must be. But John and I are trying to find out who did those terrible things to her."

"I've written a couple of stories for our paper about Maria," I said, "and now we're trying to follow some leads that may help determine who killed her. We need your help."

"My help?" Gabriel said. "No, I cannot help you. Maybe God can help you but I cannot. We came to America to live in peace. No peace here. I have nothing now. Nothing but this machine I sit on. And it is not mine."

"Can we just talk to you for a minute or so?" I said.

Gabriel Rios squeezed the steering wheel with both hands and looked again around the warehouse, and then his eyes shifted to the ceiling before returning to us. We could hear the big fans blowing and the workers speaking Spanish in the background.

"I told police everything I know," Gabriel said. "Everything. You ask questions and I'll answer. My break is over in a minute or two. Go ahead. You ask."

"Mr. Rios, did Maria ever go into Albany?" Abby said. "Did she ever go swimming in a creek? It's called the Kinchafoonee."

"No, no, no," Gabriel said. "She never leave without me. I never take her there. Don't even know about such creek. Never, never, never leave the farm without me."

"I understand, Mr. Rios," Abby said. "I understand."

"Before she disappeared that day," I said, "did you notice anybody – people you didn't know – coming around the farm? Any unusual people?"

"Saw no one like you are talking about," Gabriel said. "Saw no one."

"Anything at all out of the ordinary before she went missing?" Abby said.

"Out of what?" Gabriel said.

"Anything different," Abby said. "Did you see anything on the farm that you weren't used to seeing leading up to the day she disappeared?"

"Think hard, Gabriel," I said. "Because any little detail can turn out to be important. Think hard."

"No, nothing I saw was different," Gabriel said. "Just all of us here working every day. Working hard. We do the same every day. We're all from Nicaragua. We came for peace in America. Maria found no peace here."

"Think about the day she disappeared," Abby said. "That very day. Did you see anything while you were working that was unusual?"

"She was working by me," Gabriel said. "She always worked next to me in the fields. It was the same in Nicaragua. That day she didn't come back, she was by me. Always that way."

Gabriel pulled his hands away from the steering wheel and leaned his head back and was looking at the ceiling again as if there were answers written there. The pause continued for several seconds. Then his eyes refocused on us.

"I did see something that morning on the farm," Gabriel said. "Saw for first time same day she was gone. I didn't tell no one. Didn't tell police. Only remember now."

"What did you see that day?" Abby said.

"I tell you," Gabriel said. "I remember now. Only Mr. Walker's trucks drive through the fields. That day – now I remember – someone else drove through the fields. Someone else. It came close to Maria. And stopped near her."

"Who came close to Maria?" Abby said. "Who was it? What kind of vehicle were they in? Who did you see?"

"I saw no one's face," Gabriel said. "They drove by her three times. Jesus, Joseph, Mary. Three times."

"How many people in the vehicle?" I said.

"I only see two," Gabriel said. "Only two."

"Did they speak to Maria?" Abby said. "Did you talk to her about what happened?"

"She said the men looked at her, smiled and said nothing," Gabriel said. "Then drove away."

"White or black men?" I said. "Or brown?"

"She did not say," Gabriel said.

"Did you ask?" Abby said.

"No, I not ask," Gabriel said. "I not ask her how they look."

"What kind of vehicle was it?" I said. "What were the men driving?"

"A big van," Gabriel said. "Yes, a big van."

"What kind of van?" Abby said. "Ford? Chevy? What kind was it, Mr. Rios? This is very important. Think hard."

Gabriel Rios grabbed the forklift's steering wheel again and now looked to the concrete floor of the warehouse before answering Abby's question. There was another pause of several seconds.

"A Chevy van," he said. "Yes, I am sure. A Chevy van stopped next to my Maria. Whoever it was, looked at Maria. Then drove away."

"Do you remember what color the van was?" I said.

"Yes, yes," Gabriel said. "I remember now. Same color as those to-mato plants. Same color."

"Green?" I said.

"Green," Gabriel said. "For sure it was green. Same color."

CHAPTER 19

Shiloh Felton grew up in a trailer park with other poor white families and the best times he had were when his father wasn't home. Shiloh was the only child of Elmore and Esther Felton. His mother used to say that one suffering child is enough for any family. Having any more would just compound the suffering, she said. Shiloh understood this at an early age.

Esther wanted to name her son Shiloh, a name that means *peaceful*. Sometimes life's beginning is unfamiliar to its end.

Elmore Felton told his son stories about the black cemetery near their trailer park outside of Albany. He told Shiloh that ghosts would arise from the cemetery and cut the throat of any white boy or girl who wasn't asleep by nine each night. Elmore told Shiloh this when he was five.

Shiloh cried every time his father told him this story. And every time Shiloh cried, his father laughed loud enough to wake the dead. He kept telling it, just the same.

Elmore was a good car mechanic when he wasn't drunk. Sometimes he would work a whole day and stay sober. It wasn't often. He drank moonshine his brother made down in the small South Georgia town of Homerville. He drank from a plastic jug he called "My Good Friend." He never spoke about Shiloh or his wife with such affection.

Shiloh's mother wanted to work outside of the home once he began attending school. Elmore wouldn't allow it. The family had little money but he still wouldn't allow it.

"Ain't no woman of mine gonna do what they wanna do," Elmore said. "Ain't gonna have you runnin' all over town. Stay here where you belong. You're my woman, goddamnit."

Elmore used his open right hand to slap Shiloh for the first time when he was four and accidentally spilled a class of milk during supper. He slapped Shiloh again as the boy cried from being slapped the first time. The two slaps felt like a five-pound bee had stung him. Shiloh's face turned red then blue.

Elmore took another drink of "My Good Friend," and said, "Boy, when you gonna grow up?"

The beatings became as predictable as Elmore's drinking. When he hit Esther, she did her best not to cry in front of Shiloh, but it wasn't always possible.

At thirteen, Shiloh had earned money helping a neighbor repair a fence. He then bought a transistor radio. One night around eight in his room, he was listening to Little Richard sing *Tutti-Frutti*. His father kicked open the bedroom door.

"I don't want you listenin' to that goddamn shit! You hear me, *boy?* You're a white boy. We don't listen to that shit."

Elmore slapped Shiloh twice, snatched the transistor radio from him and threw it at the only window in the room. The radio landed outside of the trailer. Shiloh's small window now had a hole it.

"Don't ever bring that thing in my house again, boy. That god-damn shit."

Elmore never replaced the broken window. In the winter, Shiloh taped a white T-shirt over the hole to keep out cold air. Shiloh never asked his father to fix the window. He never asked his father anything.

Shiloh was seventeen in 1968 when he dropped out of high school and moved out of his family trailer. He lived with friends, spent some time with an uncle, and sometimes slept in a car he bought with what he earned working construction. He was good with his hands. They were strong like his arms and back.

He never served in the military during the Vietnam War, but years later he joined the Georgia National Guard where he met Pearl in Honduras. They became drinking buddies. They smoked pot and sometimes snorted cocaine together. Pearl introduced Shiloh to Senator Whitfield when he made his fact-finding trip to Honduras.

All three enjoyed the facts they learned about young Honduran prostitutes. Pearl began calling him "High-Low Shiloh" because when he snorted cocaine, he sometimes talked loud and other times talked low. He stayed stoned most of the time in Honduras. But he wasn't the only one who did.

A few weeks before he returned to Georgia in the summer of 1982, his father beat his mother to death with a tire iron at the family trailer. She had hidden "My Good Friend" after Elmore had been drunk for the fourth day in a row. Neighbors notified the police after hearing Esther scream.

Elmore fired his twelve-gauge shotgun at the patrol car as it arrived at the family home. He re-loaded and rushed the two officers. Elmore was shot three times in the chest and bled to death near the same spot where he had thrown Shiloh's transistor radio several years earlier.

Shiloh moved back into the family trailer where the hole in his bedroom window remained unrepaired. He found more construction work and a few nights each week drank Jack Daniels with Pearl at the Monkey Palace, where he met Big Foot. He lived alone in the trailer where he swept the floor and emptied the trash every other month.

Once a month he paid a prostitute that worked as a waitress at Joe Cellar's, a downtown bar near the Flint River. She was in her thirties. No matter how much liquor and how many prostitutes, he remained haunted by the fury that ran through his Felton blood.

Six months before Maria Rios' body was discovered, Shiloh was drinking with Pearl and Big Foot at the Monkey Palace. It was a hard time for Shiloh. He got into a fist fight with his supervisor at his last construction job. Shiloh won the fight but lost his job. He was drinking up what money he had left. His life was as tattered as the broken window in his bedroom. He had yet to fix it.

Pearl and Big Foot made Shiloh an offer that night over liquor at the Monkey Palace. They offered him a job. He could earn more in two nights then he could in a month building houses. Shiloh was interested. They said it was simple. Anyone could do it, but they wanted him. They knew things had been tough on him and they wanted to give Shiloh an opportunity to make some "real money." They said he deserved a better life after what he had been through.

Shiloh listened to their offer as he downed the third Jack Daniels over ice in five minutes. He agreed to the job before he was told what it was.

It's simple, they said. All Shiloh had to do was deliver the shipments by van a few times a month. He was to be a driver. That's all. The shipments would be delivered at night and sometimes in the early morning. They would provide the van.

Shiloh ordered his fourth drink and asked the two men when he could begin his new job. He was ready. He needed the money. Soon, they said.

CHAPTER 20

The same day we interviewed Gabriel Rios at the vegetable ware-house in Mitchell County, we went to the Monkey Palace looking to do the same with Big Foot. It was time to question him about what we had seen and heard on the creek. And about the green van.

It was around seven that evening when we arrived at the nightclub. We found a table and ordered two beers. The late-night crowd was arriving. Sugar Baby was behind the bar mixing and serving drinks. Waitresses in short black and white skirts were doing the same. You could see amble breasts.

"Band on the Run," a song by Paul McCartney and Wings, was playing on the eight-track. *Well, the undertaker drew a heavy sigh/Seeing no one else had come/And a bell was rimnging on the village square/For the rabbits on the run.*

Our beers came as we looked around the bar for Big Foot but didn't see him. I didn't want to approach Pearl. I had had enough of him for a while. We didn't see him, either.

"The green van is the key, John. It must be. You saw it in the park-ing lot here that morning. Now we know Gabriel Rios saw it. Whoever was in it was interested in Maria Rios. Maybe they took her. Maybe whoever was in the green van took her away from her uncle. Took her away from the farm. They killed her."

"We don't know if it's the same van. The one I saw and the one Gabriel saw. It could be different vans."

"Could be. But I doubt it. That may explain the girls you saw on the beach that afternoon with Pearl. The day Skeeter took you fishing."

"How's that?" I said.

"If that van took away Maria Rios, it could take away other girls too. The ones on the creek. Don't you think?"

"Maybe. Maybe you're right. That could be what the *shipment* is," I said. "It's not drugs. It's girls. Young girls."

"Shipment?"

"Yeah, shipment. Remember when we were hiding behind the shed on the creek? We heard Pearl and Big foot use that word. Don't you remember?"

"That's right. You're right. Now I remember. So they're shipping girls, John. Is that what's happening here? Those assholes got to be stopped."

"Abby, I don't know. But I got a pretty good idea of what could happen to kidnapped girls. Sex. It's sex."

"It's not sex, John. That's what you and I have. They're raped. If that happened to Maria, she was just a child. Just a child, John."

"Those girls are being sold, Abby. The ones I saw with Pearl. Maria, too. I bet those girls are being sold. Sexual slavery. That's what it is."

"God, John we've got to stop it. We've got to."

While we were talking, I continued to look throughout the nightclub and to the door every time someone entered the Monkey Palace. I wanted to talk to Big Foot. I wanted to ask him about his relationship with Pearl.

"I'll be right back," I said.

"Where you going?"

"Not far. Just want to take a look around and see if Big Foot is here. That's all."

"John, just watch what you say to him. You don't know where this thing is headed. And who has done what. Just be careful."

"Always."

I walked through the Monkey Palace twice. Every table was full. There were a few empty barstools. Then I opened the back door and looked at the parking lot. Did the same out front. I saw no green van. Then I returned to Abby.

"No sign of Big Foot or Pearl," I said. "Didn't see a green van, either."

"How about our senator? Senator Whitfield. Did you see him?"

"No, not this time."

"Do you think he's involved in this, John? The senator, I mean."

"Abby, we don't know yet what *this* is. Do I think he had something to do with Maria Rios's disappearance and death? Anything is possible. You know that. No surprises. Never."

I saw three empty barstools near where Sugar Baby was pouring drinks.

"Let's go to the bar and talk to Sugar Baby," I said. "You come with me."

"Let's go."

We took two seats together and watched Sugar Baby pour two Manhattans for a couple of men in suits and ties. The men lifted their glasses for a toast and one of them spoke.

"Here's to drinking a Manhattan," the man said. "A Manhattan is like a woman's breasts. Three is too many and one is not enough."

I had never heard the Manhattan joke before and had to laugh. It was funny. Abby did not laugh. Sugar Baby laughed with the two men who were drinking Manhattans. Then Sugar Baby approached Abby and me.

"John Maynard of the *Albany Chronicle*," Sugar Baby said. "How you doin' tonight, my man? And who's the pretty girl with you?"

"Sugar Baby, this is Abby Sinclair. We work together."

Sugar Baby wiped his right hand with the white towel that was draped over his right shoulder, then extended his hand to Abby.

"Pleasure is mine, Abby," Sugar Baby said. "Good to see you here at the Palace. What can I get for you?"

"Two Buds," I said.

"Comin' up," he said.

Sugar Baby pulled two bottles of Budweiser from the cooler, popped the tops and served the beer to us on two blue coasters that said, "There's No Palace Like the Monkey Palace. Where Everybody's King or Queen."

"The first two are on me," Sugar Baby said. "That's for bringin' Abby to the bar so I could meet her. You did good, John Maynard. Real good."

"Can't help it if I'm lucky," I said.

Sugar Baby smiled as he scanned the bar for other customers ready to order drinks. He used the towel to clean part of the bar next to us. Then I spoke again.

"Sugar Baby, you seen Big Foot tonight?"

"Nope. Says he's gonna check in sometime tonight before I shut it down. It could be one before he comes in. Hard to say with Big Foot. Sometimes he says he's comin', but I don't see him until I open again the next day. He'll show up eventually. Always does."

"Got a question for you," I said.

"Yeah, I figured," Sugar Baby said. "Go ahead."

"Do you know anybody that drives a green Chevy van and comes in here? A regular customer maybe."

"Don't know for sure. Can't say. Once I get here, I don't look out in the parking lot. Too busy makin' drinks. Know what I mean?"

"Yeah, Sugar Baby," I said. "I know what you mean."

"Why you ask that question?" he said.

"We're working on a story for the paper," I said. "That's all. There's a green van involved and we're trying to find it."

"What kind of story?" Sugar Baby said.

I took a drink from my beer, and he looked at Abby for an answer.

"We'd rather not say at this point," Abby said. "Right, John?"

"Yeah, we don't know what we have," I said. "Not yet anyway."

"You wrote about that dead girl they found up the road," Sugar Baby said. "Green van got somethin' to do with her?"

"Could be," I said. "I saw it here one morning. Same morning I saw Big Foot and Senator Whitfield."

"Morning?" Sugar Baby. "What time was it?"

"Around seven I guess," I said. "Abby dropped me off to get my car."

"Why do you think the van is connected with the girl?" Sugar Baby said. "The dead one."

"We'd rather not say right now, Sugar Baby," Abby said. "We can't say."

"You think Big Foot and the senator have some connection with the girl they found?" Sugar Baby said. "Is that what you two think?"

"We're not saying that at all," I said. "I just wanted to ask Big Foot the same question I asked you. I just want to ask about the van. That's all."

"I've known Big Foot for years," Sugar Baby said. "Ain't nothin' but a good man. Always treated me good. Dang if he ain't gonna leave me the Monkey Palace in his will. Nothin' but a good man."

"I understand, Sugar Baby," I said. "We're just trying to figure out who around here owns a green van. That's all."

"My daddy used to tell me," Sugar Baby said, "to be careful what you're lookin' for, you might not like it when you find it."

"I've heard that too, Sugar Baby," I said. "Sure have."

CHAPTER 21

The day after we spoke to Sugar Baby at the Palace, we went to visit Skeeter, the boy who shot squirrels from his bike. We wanted to ask him about a witch tree along the creek. The one Pearl and Big Foot mentioned while we were hiding behind the shed near the longhouse.

Maybe it was something that would help us understand what was happening along the creek and if what was happening there was connected to the beating and killing of Maria Rios. Skeeter knew the area. Maybe he knew something about a witch tree. We thought it was worth a try.

We drove to Skeeter's house and pulled into his driveway. He was in the front yard putting air into the back tire of his red bike. Three squirrel tails were now tied to the handlebars. Another productive morning of hunting, I thought. He saw us arrive but continued working on the tire. We parked and walked toward him.

"Shot any squirrels today?" I said

"Yep, don't you see those tails?" Skeeter said. "They fresh today. Still got blood on 'em. Then my horse gave out on me."

"That can be a problem," I said. "I hate it when that happens to John Wayne."

"I hate it when it happens to me," Skeeter said.

He finished pumping air into his tire then stood up and looked at us.

"Who's the girl?" Skeeter said.

"The girl can talk and my name is Abby Sinclair. Good to meet you, Skeeter. I'm a reporter, too, with the *Albany Chronicle*. I've heard a lot of good things about you from John."

Abby extended her hand to shake Skeeter's. He looked at me then at her. He hesitated a few moments than shook her hand. He seemed surprised that the girl could shake hands. Then he spoke to her.

"You wanna go squirrel huntin'? How 'bout fishin'? Or do you just ask questions like this guy here?"

"That's right, I just ask questions," Abby said. "And I write stories. Just like John. We do the same thing."

Abby had a big beautiful smile when she said that. It stayed on her for several moments. It was the kind of smile that first captivated me.

"No more questions," Skeeter said, "School's out for summer. I done told John that."

"Skeeter, we just got one question for you, that's all," I said. "One simple, easy question."

"Dang it, I knew it was comin'. What is it? Go ahead and ask. You're here anyway."

"Have you ever heard of a witch tree out there on the creek?" Abby said. "It could be back there where you and John saw those girls on the beach the other day. In all of those woods."

"Witch tree?" Skeeter said. "You mean the kind that flies on a broom at night? Ain't no such thing as a witch. You two been drinkin'? That's how my uncle talks when he drinks brown liquor. God, he loves it."

"No, Skeeter, we haven't been drinking," I said. "Abby said witch tree not *witch.*"

"What does that mean?" Skeeter said. "*Witch tree?* We got pine, oak, cedar – ain't no such thing as a witch tree."

"Skeeter, we're not sure what it means," Abby said. "But it could help us find out who killed the girl you found. Who killed Maria Rios."

"That's right, Skeeter," I said. "We heard two men talking about it at the creek. One of the men we saw that day with the girls. The day you took me fishing."

"How's a tree gonna tell us who kilt her?" Skeeter said. "Trees can't talk. Never heard one say a word. Least they don't ask questions like you two."

"We don't know, Skeeter," I said. "That's what we're trying to figure out. That's why we're here. We need your help."

"Skeeter, have you ever heard of anyone talking about a witch tree on that property?" Abby said. "Think hard. You may be able to help us."

"No, I ain't," Skeeter said. "Heard lots of other things. Hear things all the time. Nobody said nothin' 'bout a witch tree."

"Can you think of anything in those woods – anything – that reminds you of a witch?" Abby said.

Skeeter walked around his bike and with his right hand pressed on each tire checking it for the proper amount of air. A cowboy has to take care of his horse. Several moments passed before he spoke.

"Well, Daddy says there's slaves buried back there," Skeeter said. "Says if you go back there, they might come out of their graves and snatch you up. Might take you back in the graves with 'em. That's what my daddy says. He called 'em slave-ghosts. I know it's just a story. I don't believe any of it."

"Did he ever say anything about a witch tree?" I said.

"Nope, never did," Skeeter said. "But I reckon if you find a ghost, you might find a witch tree. Don't you reckon?"

"Could be, Skeeter," I said. "Could be."

"Skeeter, we've got to get back in there and look," Abby said, "to see if we can find that cemetery. We've got to find out where those slaves were buried. Maybe there's something back there that can help us."

"We've just got to avoid that beach and house," I said. "How can we get there, Skeeter? We don't want run into Pearl."

"I'll take you there," Skeeter said. "I know a way in those woods. They won't see us. I promise you."

"No, we don't want to get you involved in all of this, Skeeter," Abby said. "Just tell us the best way to get there."

"Involved?" Skeeter said. "I was the one who found her. Now I know her name. Purty name, too. Maria. I'll take you there. I know how to get back there and you don't. I wanna help. She wasn't much older than me."

Skeeter walked close to us, only a foot or so away. He looked at me and then at Abby. His stare was stubborn. Reminded me of Mickey at the newsroom. Twenty seconds passed.

"Abby, what do you think?" I said.

"I think we need a guide, and he's the best around here."

"Okay, Skeeter, now what are you going to tell your mom?" I said.

"Dang it, that ain't a problem," Skeeter said. "Same as last time. I ain't tellin' her I'm goin' fishin with a girl."

"That's right, Skeeter," Abby said. "I'll catch more fish than you and John combined. You can tell her that, too."

Skeeter smiled and looked at Abby, said nothing and walked into his house. Skeeter stayed inside about as long as it took him to put a cricket on a fish hook.

The three of us got in my car and drove to the creek. We stopped at his pa pa's friend's house on Uncle Jim's Lane. We got in the same johnboat Skeeter and I had fished from earlier. The Kinchafoonee was the familiar brown and smooth as we eased away from the dock.

"You got a plan, Skeeter?" Abby said. "How are we going to get back there without being seen?"

"I know a way," he said. "Up yonder past that beach there's a deer trail. Where they come from the woods to drink. We can pull the boat out of the water. We can hide it. I'll show you where the trail is."

"I like your plan, Skeeter," Abby said. "Let's do it."

Skeeter ran the boat in the middle of the Kinchafoonee and in about fifteen minutes we passed the little beach where we had seen Pearl and the young girls. The whole time we saw two other johnboats with two fishermen each. I didn't recognize any of them but we all waved just the same. Skeeter slowed the boat as he looked for the deer trail.

I grabbed Abby's right hand before saying this to her.

"Didn't think you wanted to come back here after seeing that water moccasin up close."

"I don't think about that snake anymore, John. All I think about is finding out who killed Maria Rios. If they're killing girls out here, we need to stop it."

"I'm with you Abby," I said. "I'm always with you."

A couple of hundred yards beyond the beach was when Skeeter pointed to the bank.

"See, I told you where it was," Skeeter said. "Just like I said. We can get back in there on that trail. Maybe we'll find that dang witch tree you're lookin' for."

Skeeter eased the boat onto the bank, and Abby and I got out first and held the boat steady while Skeeter got out of it. The three of us pulled the boat behind a tall thicket of blackberry and honeysuckle bushes. It was now hidden from anyone on the creek. Skeeter was satisfied with where we hid the boat and looked at Abby and smiled big.

"Purty strong for a girl. My momma could do that. She could pull that boat like you."

"Pretty strong for anybody," Abby said. "Boy or girl. Sounds like you got a good mother. Better take good care of her."

"I reckon I already do."

Skeeter kept the smile on his face and shook his head up and down in agreement. Then he took the lead on the trail with Abby in the middle.

"Stay behind me and look out for water moccasins," Skeeter said. "They won't hurt you unless you step on 'em. The long skinny ones won't hurt you. Talk nice to 'em."

"We're right here, Skeeter," I said. "Right here with you."

"Where's this trail lead?" Abby said.

"Don't know for sure," Skeeter said. "We 'bout to find out. Maybe ghosts. Maybe witches."

The trail was about three-feet wide and bordered by thick green underbrush, tall pines, and a few large water oaks with Spanish moss. It ran parallel with the creek and away from the beach and longhouse. After about fifty yards it turned north deep into the woods. We were single file and quiet.

Skeeter spoke first after a few minutes of silent walking. He stopped and pointed.

"You see that? You see that up there? Do you see it?"

"What, Skeeter?" Abby said. "What is it?"

"Up there," Skeeter said. "Look up there."

"Yeah, I see it now," Abby said. "What do you think it is?"

About thirty yards ahead the land opened to a treeless area of tall grass. It was about half the size of a football field. I could see a structure, a building of some sort. Maybe an old log cabin or a shed. I couldn't tell for certain.

"Don't know what it is," Skeeter said, "but we 'bout to find out what's up there. Just be quiet and follow me."

CHAPTER 22

Skeeter slowed his pace after seeing the clearing up ahead. Abby walked a few feet from him now, and I put my right hand on her shoulder. Skeeter stopped when we entered the clearing. We moved next to him.

Now three bodies pressed against each other. Then we saw up close what we had seen from a distance.

"You reckon your witch tree lives in there?" Skeeter said. "Looks like a good home for a witch tree. That's where I would live, if I was one."

"Could be," I said. "Maybe a slave-ghost too."

The small wooden shack was in the middle of the clearing about fifty feet from the tree-line. It was of gray clapboard with a lot of rotten wood and a redbrick chimney. It looked as if it had never been painted. There was no porch but two steps led to the front door. We were facing the front door.

On the three sides we could see there were no windows. The back side of the cabin was out of our view. If someone had told me it was two-hundred years old, I'd believe them. There was no other structures in the clearing. Only the shack.

"Maybe it's a witch cabin," Skeeter said, "and ghosts live in there too. What about that?"

"Skeeter, you don't believe in witches and ghosts, do you?" Abby said.

"No, I believe in fishin' and huntin'," Skeeter said.

"No witches here," I said. "Let's take a look."

We walked to the cabin and stopped at the front-door steps. They were cracked and looked as if they would buckle with our weight on top of them. There was no doorknob or lock, but there was a hole in the middle of the door about the size of a baseball.

"I reckon we don't have to knock," Skeeter said. "Don't see a doorbell. Witches don't need a doorbell. Ghosts don't either."

"I don't think anybody's home," Abby said. "They haven't been home in a while."

I put my right hand through the hole in the door and pulled it open. There was no resistance. The cabin was one room with no furniture. Cobwebs hung thick from the ceiling. The dirt in some places looked held over from the nineteenth century and maybe before. A good home for a raccoon family, I thought.

With no windows, the light inside was that of the few minutes each day before the sun falls below the horizon. But I saw something in a corner. I walked to it for a better look.

"What is it, John?" Abby said. "What do you see?"

"You tell me what I'm seeing, Abby. You tell me."

Now the three of us were standing over the object in the corner. It appeared to be a carving about four-feet tall. The wood was smooth and white. It was shaped like a tree with bizarre limbs. Scary like a witch.

The witch carving was attached to a large wooden block. That was the only object in the cabin. The witch tree.

"Well, there it is," I said. "That must be it. That must be what Pearl and Big Foot were talking about."

"Must be what?" Abby said. "What is it?"

"The witch tree," I said. "There it is. Look at those scary limbs."

"What?" Skeeter said. "That ain't no tree. Just a piece of junk. Dang it, I knew we should've gone fishin' instead of walkin' through these woods. Dang it, I knew it all along."

"No, Skeeter, that's the witch tree," I said.

"Ain't either," Skeeter said. "Just some messed up wood. Ain't nothin' but junk."

"It's a carving," Abby said. "Somebody carved it and whether or not it's a witch tree, we'd have to ask the person who carved it."

"Who is that?" Skeeter said. "Who carved it?"

"Well, Skeeter, maybe a slave-ghost did it," I said. "Or a very talented raccoon. Or a real witch."

"You 'bout as funny as a tick on a dick...Oh, I'm sorry, Abby," Skeeter said. "I need to watch my mouth. That's what my momma tells me."

"No need to be sorry, Skeeter," Abby said. "I've heard both of those words before. Just not used in that order."

"Where'd you hear that one, Skeeter?" I said. "That's a good one."

"Reckon it wasn't from my teacher at school. She don't know nothin'. My pa pa told me that one. Tick on a dick. Now that's funny."

Abby picked up the carving but needed both hands because of the heaviness of the wooden block it was attached to. She looked at it close for a few moments and was about to return it to the same spot where she had lifted it from. Then she hesitated.

"John. Skeeter. Look at this. What is this?"

Abby sat the witch tree carving on the floor a few feet away from the spot where she had found it. On the same spot where we found the carving itself, was a silver latch attached to a large wooden slat that was part of the cabin's floor.

The latch was shiny and looked new, not of the last century but of this one. It seemed out of place in the cabin. The three of us looked at the silver latch and the floor.

"Buried treasure underneath," I said. "You think it leads to buried treasure?"

"That's right, Johnny Boy," Abby said. "Probably lots of Confederate money down there. We could take it all and travel the world."

"Johnny Boy?" Skeeter said. "Dang, is that your real name?"

"It is when I say it is," Abby said.

"Okay, I don't mess with you," Skeeter said.

I knelt on my knees and reached for the silver latch to see what was underneath the floor of the cabin. Abby and Skeeter were standing over me. I lifted the piece of the floor that the latch was attached to. Now we could see beyond the old wooden floor and into the dirt below.

The dirt was mounded and looked to have the texture of that which had been dug and re-piled.

"Abby, this must be where Pearl put the problem he and Big Foot were talking about," I said.

Then we heard the door of the cabin open. We turned to look. It was Pearl. His stare was on me. He charged across the cabin and as I stood up his face was all I could see. His liquor breath was all I could smell.

"Damn, ya boy!" Pearl said. "I told ya never to bring your sorry goddamn ass 'round here again. I told ya never go lookin' where ya shouldn't. Didn't I boy? Didn't I?"

Pearl grabbed me by my shirt with both hands and slammed me against the wall next to the witch tree. He kept his weight pressed against me and I couldn't move.

He jammed his left arm under my neck and with his right hand pulled a switchblade from his pocket and opened the knife. He pressed the blade against my nose. Like the gun I saw him carrying on the beach with the young girls, the knife had a pearl-white handle.

He cut into my nose and blood dripped on my lips. It wasn't a deep cut, but I tasted my own blood.

"I don't know if I'm gonna cut ya nose off or ya balls," Pearl said. "I'm cuttin' somethin' off. Then maybe ya won't come back here again, boy."

I struggled to breathe but my eyes were working. I could see Abby approaching Pearl as his rage was fixated on me. She had the carved statue of the witch tree in her hands. She was holding it by the top-end and extended high above her head.

I knew what she was going to do. If she failed, he might kill us all.

Pearl pressed the knife into my nose again and Abby swung hard hitting him on the right temple with the heavy wooden platform the carving was attached to. Pearl released his hold on me and turned to Abby.

His right knee buckled as if he was drunk and about to fall. Blood was running thick from his temple. He was still standing.

"You little whore," Pearl said. "Ya ain't nothin' but a bitch…"

She hit him again in the same spot and this time he fell to the floor like an anvil dropped from a tall pine. He lay still but moaning. Blood flowed from his head onto the silver latch that I used to lift the wooded piece. The latch was turning red.

"Is he dead?" Skeeter said. "You hit 'im hard for a girl. Hard for a boy, too. Is he dead?"

"Did I John? Did I kill him? He's not dead is he?"

"No, he's not dead," I said, "but we're going to be if we don't get out of here. He's just asleep."

Abby dropped the witch tree statue, and we ran out of the cabin and back to the deer trail that led to the creek. We kept running when we got onto the trail. We didn't look back. We didn't stop running until we got to the johnboat.

We pulled the boat back into the water and got in. Skeeter ran full throttle until we returned to where I had parked my car. I looked behind us for Pearl but didn't see him. No one talked until we were driving away from the Kinchafoonee and back to Albany.

"You sure you're a girl?" Skeeter said. "Girls don't do that. You weren't scared?"

"I'm certain I'm a girl," Abby said. "And yes, I was scared. Weren't you?"

"Dang sure was," Skeeter said.

"Abby did what she had to do," I said. "She saved us. All of us."

"I reckon she did," Skeeter said. "Ain't nobody goin' to mess with you. They goin' call you Super Woman. Like Super Man."

"Now, Skeeter, stay away from the creek," Abby said. "We're going to find out what's happening out there and stop it. But for now you stay around your house where it's safe. Okay?"

"Yeah, okay," Skeeter said. "If I need to knock somebody out, I'll just call you."

"That's a deal," Abby said.

I pulled into Skeeter's driveway, and he ran inside his house. Then we drove to my house. I got a beer and poured Abby a glass of Merlot. We sat together on my sofa, and I played a Van Morrison album. We were doing our best to relax and breathe easy. And it was hard.

"Is he dead, John? I didn't mean to kill him, but I wasn't going to let him hurt you or Skeeter."

"No, he's not dead and you did what you had to do to protect us. He'll have a headache for a while and be mad as hell, but you didn't kill him. He may try to kill us later."

"You sure he's not dead?"

"Sure I'm sure. I'm sure of something else, too."

"What's that?"

"I'll never mess with you. Like Skeeter said, 'You sure you're a girl?'"

"What do you think?"

"A damn fine girl, I'd say. A helluva woman. I'd say that, too."

I leaned and whispered in her ear. "I love you."

"I love you more, my very. You know I love you very much."

"Well, you make a helluva bodyguard."

"Only for you, Johnny Boy. Only for you."

"And Skeeter."

"That's right. And Skeeter."

She raised her glass for a toast and we both took a drink.

"I have an awful thought, John. Just awful."

"I said he's not dead, and he's not going to die. Probably not even possible to kill that man."

"Not about him."

"What then?"

"What's underneath that floor, John? That cabin floor."

"It did look as if somebody had been digging there, and Pearl told Big Foot that he put "the problem" under the witch tree. We just don't know what the problem is. "

"There's definitely something down there that your friend Pearl didn't want us to find. Don't you think it's odd he shows up at the cabin same time we're there? How did he know we were there? Did he see our boat? Or does he come out to that old cabin on a regular basis? Maybe prays to the witch tree."

"Abby, I don't have the answers to any of your questions. All good questions. But I do know one thing."

"What's that?"

"He ain't a friend of mine."

I tapped the side of my nose where Pearl had cut me with his knife. It was not deep enough for snitches. Abby had helped me clean it and put ice on it.

"I'm sorry about your nose, John. It could've been worse. He could've cut off you know what."

"Yeah, I remember exactly what he said. That would've been bad for both of us. I don't want to lose those."

"What's under that cabin, John? Think. Speculate. What could be under there? What was Pearl protecting?"

"Drugs. Money. What else do people hide? These guys could be dealing in a lot of drugs and money."

"People hide people, John. These guys could be hiding people. Dead people. Dead girls."

"What? What are you saying, Abby?"

"Could someone, maybe Pearl, put a body down there, John? Put a body under the witch tree? The body of a teenage girl?"

"Someone could put a small body or a big body. It depends on how long you have to dig."

"There's been one body found around here," Abby said. "One teenage girl tortured and killed and dumped off Palmyra Road. She might not be the only one. Maria Rios might not be the only one. There might be others."

"So you think there's a dead girl under that cabin? Under the witch tree?"

"I don't know, but I do know we need to go back and find out. We need to go back there. Dead girl. Or dead girls."

"Let's tell the cops, Abby. Let them go back to the cabin."

"Tell them what? That there's an old cabin in the woods with a witch tree inside? You think that'll get them a search warrant from a Dougherty County judge?"

"We'll tell the cops, Detective McGill, everything we know."

"No, John. We go back. We do it ourselves."

CHAPTER 23

Senator Jefferson Beauregard Whitfield's first visit to the longhouse on the Kinchafoonee Creek was about six months before the body of Maria Rios was found. He returned several times and was always satisfied with what his money could buy him. The last time he visited was the night Maria was tortured and killed.

He was the most well-known customer on the creek.

On that night Whitfield had spoken at Whispering Pines Baptist Church in Albany where about three hundred people attended a worship service. His topic was family values and how he lives them daily.

It was the Republican Party mantra and one which Whitfield was proud to proclaim.

He left the church about eight-thirty and drove alone to the creek. Two armed men were stationed at the entrance of the private property at the end of Uncle Jim's Lane. Whitfield stopped his silver Ford LTD, spoke to the men and continued to the longhouse. They recognized him and knew he was coming that night.

There were about ten vehicles parked near the longhouse. He parked his car, spoke to the armed man at the door, and went inside.

The senator approached Pearl who was sitting at a wooden table smoking a fat joint with Shiloh Felton. There were a few other men in the big room doing the same. All were drinking liquor served by topless women. The lights were dim as Whitfield sat down at the table next to Pearl.

A big breasted woman brought the senator a glass of Dewar's on ice. She knew he liked good Scotch. He had ordered it several times before that night.

"Been waitin' on ya," Pearl said. "Got somethin' for ya. Me and Hi-Low got somethin' for ya. I know ya goin' like her."

The senator shook hands with Pearl and Shiloh. He knew them both from his time in Honduras and from his frequent visits to the longhouse.

"I've been speaking about family values tonight," Whitfield said. "One of my favorite topics. Had everybody in the whole church listening."

"I got your family values hangin'," Pearl said.

Pearl grabbed his crotch with his right hand and shook it five times. Shiloh laughed then started coughing as he was in the middle of a long hit on the joint. It took him a few seconds to recover. Smoke engulfed the three men. He handed the joint to Pearl, who took a strong hit himself. They called it "one-hit shit."

"Dang, Pearl, you tore my ass up," Shiloh said. "That's some funny shit. Got your family values hangin'. That shit's funny. And this is some damn good one-hit shit."

"Hi-Low, you know that's all we got at the Kinchafoonee Gentleman's Club," Pearl said. "One-hit shit and a lot of other good shit. Ain't that right, J. B.?"

"I would have to vote yes to that," Whitfield said. "I am among real patriots out here. You provide a needed service to the community, Pearl. You'll probably receive a medal one day for all your good works. I'll recommend one for you when I return to Washington."

"Senator, ya sure know how to say the right thing," Pearl said. "Ya got a lot of good words. Nothin' but good words. Always full of goat shit. Full to the brim."

Whitfield took the joint from Pearl, hit it hard and washed it down with Dewar's. He held the joint a few seconds then hit it again. The senator took another drink of Dewar's then passed the joint back to Shiloh.

The waitress returned with another Dewar's for Whitfield, and she pressed her breasts against the senator's thick dark hair. He smiled and closed his eyes.

Pearl opened a small silver container and from it formed three lines of cocaine on the wooden table. He then took a hundred dollar bill from a black leather money bag that was attached to his belt. He rolled the bill tight and gave it to the senator.

"The first one's for you," Pearl said. "It's the biggest. It'll get you ready. If you're not already ready."

"I'm always ready," the senator said.

Whitfield snorted the line and chased it with the Dewar's. He passed the hundred dollar bill to Shiloh, who snorted the second line. Then Pearl snorted the third. He put three more lines on the table and each man had another hit of blow.

"You been servin' the people again today, senator?" Shiloh said. "I know you have."

"I always do," Whitfield said. "That's my job. This is a great country, Shiloh. And Georgia's a great state. The greatest of them all."

"And another inspirational speech," Pearl said.

"I use it a lot," Whitfield said. "I did tonight. I talked about family values at the church. One of my favorite subjects. The people love me when I talk about family values. You know how committed I am to family values? I know you know it."

"Dang sure do, senator," Pearl said. "That's why ya came here tonight. We're one big happy family out here."

"Sure is," Whitfield said. "I believe in family values wherever I go."

"Ya gonna love who I got for ya tonight," Pearl said. "She's just ya kind of family member. Hi-Low made it all possible. He's a dang good business partner."

"Thank you, Shiloh," Whitfield said. "Your country is indebted to you."

"My country is what to me?" Shiloh said. "What's that mean?"

"It just means thank you," Whitfield said. "Thank you for getting her here."

"Okay, well, my country is welcome," Shiloh said. "You're always welcome, Senator Whitfield. I'm a patriot just like you."

"Now tell me what you got for me, Pearl," Whitfield said.

"She's a real family girl," Pearl said. "Just how ya like 'em. All dark skin and dark hair. Smooth skin. Her nipples poke out just right. Hadn't been used much at all. Almost fresh she is. Almost. Shiloh done tried her out."

"I can't wait to meet her," Whitfield said. "I can't stay long. I promised my wife I wouldn't be late tonight."

Senator Whitfield stood up from the table where he had smoked the joint and snorted cocaine and pulled his black leather wallet from his jacket pocket. He was wearing the standard dress for a U.S. senator. Expensive blue suit, starched white shirt, and red and blue striped tie. Perfect for a campaign ad.

He was inconspicuous in the Kinchafoonee Gentleman's Club. Other customers who were lawyers, preachers, and businessmen stopped in for fun dressed the same way. Sometimes officers from the APD came out and enjoyed the entertainment. Like Whitfield, they usually didn't stay long.

"I think this is what we agreed on for tonight," Whitfield said. "You usually give me the government discount."

Whitfield placed two crisp one hundred dollar bills on the table in front of Pearl. He finished his Dewar's and set the empty glass near the money. Pearl picked up the money and placed it in his black money bag. The deal was done. Whitfield was ready.

"Yes, sir, this is just right for government work, senator," Pearl said. "We're just glad ya came out for a little family fun. Always good to see ya here at the Club."

"What room number tonight?" Whitfield said.

"Lucky seven," Pearl said. "She's twice that old. Just like ya like 'em. Only twice that old."

"What's her name?" Whitfield said.

"Angel. Her name is Angel," Pearl said.

"The last three were called Angel," Whitfield said. "That's a popular name here on the creek. There was a lot of talk about angels at Whispering Pines Baptist Church tonight."

"Yeah, but we got the best kind out here, don't we Pearl?" Shiloh said.

"They're all angels out here," Pearl said. "We're just doin' the Lord's work here. Just like we did down in Honduras. Right, senator?"

"That's right, and I think we had a few named Angel down there," Whitfield said.

"Oh, yeah, that's right," Pearl said. "Back when we were keepin' America safe from the commies. Not one commie made here, did they senator?"

"That's right," Whitfield said. "Not one."

Whitefield then held his hand out in front of Pearl. He said nothing but looked at both Pearl and Shiloh.

"Oh, shit, I'll be a drunken preacher," Pearl said. "Almost forgot."

"I think you did forget," Whitfield said.

Pearl opened again his money bag and reached to the bottom. He pulled out a silver key and handed it to Whitfield. The senator held it a few inches from his face as if he couldn't tell what it actually was.

"This was the best part about fighting the communists," Whitfield said. "Wasn't it, Pearl?"

"God bless America," Pearl said.

"Yes, God bless America," Whitfield said.

"Now remember, senator," Pearl said. "The room is number seven. Room seven. Go to heaven in seven. Heaven seven. Seven takes you to heaven."

"Don't worry, I remember all the important things," Whitfield said.

"And one more thing," Pearl said.

"What's that?"

"Like I said, she's almost fresh," Pearl said. "I know how ya like to wrestle with 'em sometimes. Make 'em tough. Keep her fresh, if ya can."

"I'll be gentle this time," Whitfield said. "I promise. For God and country."

Senator Whitfield shook hands with Pearl and Shiloh then walked to a long corridor where there were ten doors on each side. The doors were numbered one through twenty. Thick green carpet filled the hallway. It was well lit unlike where Whitfield had drunk, smoked, and snorted with Pearl and Shiloh. Two speakers provided jazz music in the corridor. Miles Davis filled the hallway.

In the middle of the corridor, two men sat at a small white folding table playing cards. Like the security at the front entrance and at the door, these two men were more than six feet tall. Thick and muscular.

There were two thirty-eight revolvers on the table.

The two men looked at Whitfield as he entered the long hall but no one spoke. They continued playing cards as the senator found room number seven. He had not been in number seven before that night. He unlocked the door and went inside.

Angel, as she was called, was naked on a king size bed. The room was lit by two long white candles sitting on nightstands on each side of the bed. The jazz music from the corridor was piped into the room. The drugs Pearl had forced into her made her lethargic, barely awake. But her coal-dark eyes were wide as she saw the senator walk in.

Whitfield locked the door behind him, took off his clothes and got on top of her. He said nothing as he entered her. There was no resistance from her.

He was with her much longer than he had first planned. He didn't return to his wife and children in Camilla until around midnight.

CHAPTER 24

On the same day Abby clobbered Pearl with the witch tree statute and saved Skeeter and me, she wanted to return to the shack in the woods on the creek to learn what might be buried underneath it.

It was an idea I didn't like. We could get killed out there, I thought.

"Bad idea, Abby. Very bad idea. We should tell Mickey what happened to us today. We should tell the cops. Damn, Abby, have you forgotten that Pearl was about to cut my nose off? And cut something else off. Something more important than my nose. Have you forgotten that already? You remember, don't you?"

"Yes, I remember. I was the one who saved your nose and your balls. You remember that, don't you?"

"Yeah, I do. That's exactly why we're not going back there without help. Hell, we could've gotten Skeeter hurt today. How would we feel if that had happened? We'd feel worse than shit, that's how we'd feel."

"We would've felt awful," Abby said, "but Skeeter didn't get hurt and we're not going to involve him again, John. One girl about his age – Maria Rios – did get hurt and killed. That's why we're going back to the creek. I'll go with or without you."

"It just doesn't make any sense unless you're trying to get us both killed."

"John, don't you see, your friend Pearl won't be expecting us tonight. He probably still has a headache. We need a flashlight. We need a shovel. And we need to find out if there's anything buried under that old cabin. There may be something out there that helps us find Maria's killer."

"I got a flashlight and a shovel. But you tell me how we're going to get back up the creek tonight. Inner tubes? Swim? Tell me how we're going to do it. I don't have a boat, you don't either. What's our plan?"

"Don't you have a friend that lives on that part of the creek?" Abby said. "I think I met the guy once. Doesn't he teach at Albany Junior College? Maybe he can help us. What's the guy's name? You know who I'm talking about."

Abby referred to Warren Crews, who lived on the Kinchafoonee just a mile or so from the longhouse and the shack. Warren was in his mid-thirties and did teach American literature at the local junior college. It had taken him only six years to go through three wives. He said he figured at this rate he could end up with "ten or eleven before my bobber goes under for good."

Warren was a good writer and contributed stories to fishing and hunting magazines that covered the Southeast. If he wasn't teaching, reading, writing, or screwing women, he was fishing or hunting. His emulation of Ernest Hemingway was apparent on and off the page. Hemingway was his heroic model.

He enjoyed participating in the rattlesnake roundup down in Whigham, fishing for speckled trout in the Gulf of Mexico, and fly fishing for trout in the Toccoa River in North Georgia. Warren's reputation had been enshrined in an overnight canoe trip on the Flint River south of Albany. It involved lots of tequila and pot.

His canoe mates spotted a nine-foot gator half submerged in mud and reeds along the river. They said the gator was sleeping. And they said they would buy Warren a bottle of Jose Cuervo if he jumped on top of the alligator and stayed on for ten seconds. If he stayed more than ten seconds, he'd get two bottles.

Warren didn't hesitate. After fifteen seconds, he was tossed into the mud by the gator. Not a scratch on him and the tequila did taste good.

"If you're talking about Warren Crews, he lives on the Kinchafoonee not too far from where we were today," I said. "Good guy. A lot of fun. Pretty good writer, too."

"That's him. Call him, John. He'll help us get back to that shack. Call him now, John."

"Abby, now? It's after ten. We can wait until tomorrow then I'll call him. I don't want to call this late. We need help, Abby. Let's get help tomorrow."

"What! Too late? I'll call him and go by myself, John. You're talking about how late it is when another girl could get killed? I'm not waiting."

"I just think we should wait, Abby."

"Wait for what? Another girl to be tortured and killed. Is that what we're going to wait for? Not me. I'm not waiting. *We're* not waiting."

"Like I said, we don't even know for sure what's happening out there. We do know that there's somebody out there capable of hurting us."

"There's enough evidence for me, John. I'm not waiting. If you're not going to call your friend, I'll find the number and I'll call."

"I'll call."

I called Warren Crews, and the phone rang eight times before he answered. He spoke as if he had just run a hundred yards as fast as he could. I heard the word hello as he was gasping for air.

"Warren, this is John Maynard. Are you okay?"

Ten seconds passed before Warren spoke.

"Better now that I know you're not one of my ex-wives. But I am kind of busy right now, Maynard."

"Warren, I apologize for the late call but it's important. I won't keep you long."

"Good. I'm working on my relationship with Deborah right now." Deborah was Warren's current girlfriend.

"I just got one quick question for you, Warren."

"Make it so. Deborah and I are about to reach a fuller understanding of each other."

"I understand."

In just a few seconds longer than Warren was able to stay on the back of that alligator on the Flint River, I explained to him the story we were working on. He didn't ask any questions and was probably thinking about getting back to Deborah and their relationship.

I had been in Warren's boat with him a few times about a year earlier when I was working on a feature story about his involvement in conservation efforts throughout the state. His boat and motor resembled that of the one we had been on with Skeeter.

After writing the story on Warren, I had gotten to know him better and sometimes went to his house on the creek to have beers and talk about famous writers and local politics. He was fun to be with. Had a big zest for life and was a great storyteller. He said we were welcome to use his boat tonight or any night. I wasn't surprised.

"Thanks, Warren. We'll be heading your way in a few minutes. I don't particularly like this idea but Abby is insistent. I couldn't talk her out of it."

"Doesn't Cat Stevens sing a song about some hard-headed woman?" Warren said.

"Yeah, he sure does. Been a Cat Stevens fan for a few years. And that's what I have in Abby. A hard-headed woman. Lot of other things, too."

"Well, you gotta love those kind."

"Absolutely."

After the phone conversation with Warren, I told Abby we could use his boat to return to the shack in the woods. I still thought it was a bad and even dangerous idea, but I was following her dogged lead.

"Let's go, John. We need to get back to the creek. Let's go now."

"Okay, give me a second."

I got a large flashlight and shovel from the storage closet near my backdoor. It was about ten-thirty.

"Ready now, but I still think it'd be smarter for us to wait, Abby. To get some help."

She looked at me and didn't say a word. Then she walked out my front door toward my car. I followed her with the flashlight and shovel.

CHAPTER 25

Both my gut and mind told me it would be foolish and dangerous going back to the creek tonight with Abby. That's just a dumbass idea, I thought. I didn't say it that way to Abby. She was determined.

By water, I estimated that Warren's house was about a mile or so upstream from where we were headed. And where we were headed was the deer trail that led to the shack that Skeeter had taken us to. Now we had to find it ourselves in the night's darkness.

Warren's house was a log cabin and about a fifteen-minute drive from my house. I pulled into his red-dirt driveway and saw that his green jeep was parked under a large magnolia tree covered with white blooms. He was proud of the jeep but sometimes drove it like it was being punished.

Next to the jeep was a yellow Volkswagen Beetle and on the back windshield was lettering that said, "Debbie's Bug Bites Back." That must belong to his girlfriend, I thought.

I parked, and we walked around Warren's house to the creek and his boat at the dock. There was not a light on in the house. I carried the shovel and followed Abby. She held the flashlight in her extended right arm.

"John, watch your step. Water moccasins don't like to be stepped on. And I don't either."

"Will you bite me if I step on you?"

"No, but I bet Debbie will."

"Oh, I just love it when you're trying to be funny. Especially when we could get killed by a crazy man."

"Trying to be? That was funny. You should be laughing."

"Ha . . . Ha . . . Ha . . ."

"Authentic. Very authentic."

"That's the best I can do."

"John, just stay close to me and we'll be all right. We'll be safe to-gether. We always will be."

"I'm not worried about snakes, gators, or even Debbie biting me. You know what worries me?"

"He's probably still lying down somewhere with an ice pack on his head," Abby said. "I did whack him pretty good, didn't I?"

"Twice. You whacked him twice pretty good."

"Had no choice, Johnny Boy."

"I'll never piss you off, that's for sure."

"Good. I like it when you talk like that."

Warren's gray wooden dock was about fifty yards from the back door of his cabin. We walked on square cement steps that had been placed in the yard and led to the creek. The yard itself was of lush green grass, and it included a gazebo, a couple of palm trees, and six red rose-bushes.

We could smell the roses as we walked by them. The aroma was remarkable. At the dock, we got into the boat and I laid the shovel over the middle seat as Abby sat in the front of the boat with me behind her to operate the twenty-five-horse-power motor. She pointed the flash-light at the motor as I pulled on the white-starter rope.

On the third pull, the motor turned over, and I guided the boat downstream as we eased into the middle of the Kinchafoonee.

The water was calm. There was no breeze. A typical sticky, hot summer night in South Georgia. The wind from the ride felt good on my face and for just a few moments I forgot the reason we were on the water.

"Abby, I got a question for you. Very important question."

"No, we are not turning back. We've got to do this tonight."

"I know, I know. I'm with you on this now. My question is about something else. Not about this story we're on."

"What is it?"

"Do you remember what we did at the Blue Hole last summer? It was on the Fourth of July, wasn't it?"

She turned around in the front of the boat so I could see her smile of remembrance. In the dark I could see the light in her eyes.

"Didn't I read Walt Whitman to you before we did it?" Abby said. "We found a nice soft spot in the sand away from the crowd."

"It was Whitman that did it for me. You got me all excited reading him. America is large, as Whitman said. What a great country."

"Now I remember what I read to you. It was from "Song of Myself." The words were, *The wonder is always and always how there can be a mean man or an infidel.*"

"That's it. That got me all excited."

"Oh, Johnny Boy, that was a good day on the creek for us. A lot more fun than knocking Pearl out with a witch tree statue. And if he had had his way with you, we won't be able to do that *good thing* anymore. Would we, Johnny Boy?"

"Did you have to remind me of that? I was trying to think of something fun before we get off of this boat and walk in the woods."

"Sorry, Johnny Boy, just trying to keep it light."

"Light? Ruining all my good thoughts. Shame on you."

"I have my ways."

"Oh, I know that. Just look at what we're doing."

Abby turned around to face the front of the boat again and shone the flashlight along the bank to our right. We were getting closer to where we needed to be. I stopped thinking about making love with her and focused on what we had come to do. It took a few moments to get the love-making thoughts out of my mind.

Along the route from Warren's to the deer trail there were only a couple of other homes, and with little artificial light the three-quarter moon reflected on the water, giving us more visibility in the darkness. We were silent now and heard the loud screeching of an owl on the right bank of the creek. Then we heard another owl from the left bank.

"What do you think they're saying, Abby?"

"They're saying whatever you want them to say. You decide."

"You talk like Walt Whitman. Or maybe Bob Dylan. Or maybe . . ."

"Look, John! There it is. There's the trail we were on today with

Skeeter. You see it? Do you see it?"

She had the beam of the flashlight on the trail, and I could see where we had stopped with Skeeter and hidden the boat we were using before walking to the shack. I guided Warren's boat toward the bank and the trail.

"Yeah, I got it. That's it. That's the same one we were on today."

"We need to pull the boat out of the water like we did today," Abby said. "We need to hide it like we did today. Just in case."

"We'll do it, but remember we got found anyway."

"Better to do it than not do it," Abby said.

"That sounds like something Whitman said."

"Let's forget about Whitman for a while. He didn't say it, I did."

After we hid the boat in the bushes, we began our slow walk to the shack. The cypress trees along the creek were bent and cragged, and I had found beauty in them before tonight, but now they appeared ugly and eerie. Crickets chirped in the stillness of the woods. Abby was in the lead with the flashlight. I held the shovel in both hands as if I was ready to swing it.

After about fifty feet on the trail, she stopped and pointed her light at two animal eyes probably a hundred or so yards to our right. A raccoon, I thought.

"Look. My daddy used to call those God's eyes," Abby said. "He took me camping a lot when I was little. He said when you see animals at night, with bright white eyes looking at you, it's really God watching over you."

"I like that, Abby. We need God watching over us tonight."

"Yes, we do."

We continued walking and heard the owls again. Louder this time than before. Maybe they were part of God's protection plan, too, I thought. I was willing to take help from wherever we could get it. In a few minutes, the shack came into full view.

In the clearing the moon's light cast a glow that lit the shack and the treeless ground around it. It was if the sun itself was rising, but we had hours before that would occur. I stopped at the edge of the clearing and asked Abby to do the same. I knew it was useless, but I said it anyway.

"You sure about all this. We don't have to go any farther. We can go back. We don't have to do this."

She didn't say anything. She didn't even look at me. I followed her to the shack with a tight grip on my shovel.

"Okay, lead the way," I said. "I'm right behind you."

Her steps were deliberate and straight to the front door of the old cabin. The door was opened but not all the way. She went in first and after I entered, I pushed the door open in full allowing light from the moon inside the shack.

Abby shone the flashlight in the corner of the shack where the witch tree statute was, the weapon used against Pearl. There was a pool of dried blood on the floor. It was more purple than red, and the pool was about three or four times the size of a quarter. Not a lot, but it must have been his blood from the blows Abby had delivered. Without talking, we began to do what we had come to do.

Abby put down the flashlight and moved the wooden statue to another corner of the cabin. Then the work began. I used the shovel to lift up the same piece of flooring we had lifted up earlier. Then together we pulled away four more pieces of flooring and stacked all five of them near the witch tree statue. I now had enough room to dig.

"Keep the light on the dirt," I said. "This shouldn't take long. We'll find out either way."

"John."

"What is it?"

"We're doing the right thing."

"I hope you're right."

I started digging and piling the dirt in a pile not far from the witch tree statue. The club that Abby used. She stood next to me with the light beam fixed on the work I was doing. We were silent as I dug. After about four or five minutes of shoveling, I stopped.

I saw something in the dirt. Then I smelled something.

"What's that, John? What do you see down there?"

"Looks like a black garbage bag. The big kind."

"The smell is awful. It's sickening."

"That's the smell of death, Abby. We got to get out of here."

"No, John, not yet. We got to look. As much as we don't want to, we got to look. There may be another dead girl in there but we got to look."

Then I did what I didn't want to do. I untied the top of the black bag. I was gagged by the smell and held my breath. I pushed the top of bag down a foot or so. Then I saw it.

It was the back of a man's head with what appeared to be a bullet hole in it. I would have to keep digging if I was to see more of the body. The putrid smell was too much for me to overcome. I couldn't dig anymore without a mask or something to keep the smell off me.

Then we heard the sound of a vehicle coming from the woods.

"It's him, Abby! Let's get the hell out of here. He's back. Pearl's back."

"Let's go!"

Abby ran out of the cabin with me behind her. It was the same scene that had played out earlier in the day minus Skeeter. She turned off her flashlight not wanting to give Pearl or whoever was coming a signal of where we were. The encroaching vehicle was getting closer as we reached the trail. Now we raced to the creek as the sound of the vehicle faded.

We ran the entire trail without using the flashlight, pulled the boat into the water and were gone. Abby kept the flashlight off as I guided us back to Warren's. The light from the moon helped, and I stayed in the middle of the Kinchafoonee. Neither of us spoke until we could see Warren's dock.

"I've seen dead people before," I said, "but never smelled one. God Almighty that was awful."

"Was it a girl, John? Was it a young girl like Maria Rios?"

"No, not a girl. Not a woman. A man. A white man with a hole in the back of his head. Probably a bullet hole."

"I couldn't see the bullet hole," Abby said. "Could you see his face at all? Could you describe him?"

"No, I couldn't see his face. Not the way he was turned in the bag.

I couldn't tell you if he was naked or had clothes on. Only the head, Abby."

"How old do you think he was?"

"Not old, not young. Hard to say."

"How long you think he's been dead?"

"Hell, Abby I can't say. I'm not an expert on dead bodies. That's not why the paper hired me."

"You may be one before this over."

"Hope not."

"We know one thing, John."

"What's that?"

"That's why Pearl didn't want us in that shack. He didn't want us to find what was underneath it. That's why he threatened us. He's a killer, John. He probably killed Maria Rios, too."

"We know something else," I said.

"What's that?"

"We know what 'the problem' was. The problem that Pearl and Big Foot talked about."

"You're right, John. Pearl shot the problem and buried him underneath the witch tree in the cabin. The man's a beast. The man in the bag – the dead man – is connected with Maria Rios. Somehow it's connected."

"Based on what, Abby? How do you know that?"

"Let's put it altogether, John. Maria's body is found nearby off Palmyra Road. Pearl threatened you the morning you followed Big Foot and Senator Whitfield to the creek. The morning you left the Monkey Palace. The day you and Skeeter were on the creek, you saw Pearl with those girls. Those young girls, just like Maria. Then there's the conversation we overheard between Big Foot and Pearl when he talked about the *problem* being taken care of and the witch tree. And what do you think is going on in that longhouse on the creek? Put it all together."

"Do you think Senator Whitfield is involved with young girls from Latin America? Girls like Maria Rios. You think he's connected to the man who was shot in the back of the head and buried under the shack?"

"I don't know, but I do know one thing," Abby said. "We're going to find out. We'll get to the truth out here on the creek. I promise you that."

"I believe you, Abby. I believe you."

I slowed the motor as we came to a stop at Warren's dock. We got out, secured the boat to the dock and walked for a second time that night through his backyard.

I stopped next to his rosebushes and a pulled a long, deep breath. With the aroma of the red roses, I was trying to counter the smell of death from the black bag I had dug up.

But the bullet hole in the back of the man's head was an image no rose could eliminate. As we got into my car to drive home, I could hear two owls in the distance. The sounds seemed to be coming from the old cabin on the creek. A cabin of death.

CHAPTER 26

The morning after I dug up the dead man who had a hole in his head, we drove to the APD to speak with Detective McGill. He was in charge of the murder case involving Maria Rios and needed to know what we had seen and heard the past few days on the Kinchafoonee Creek. We hoped what we had would help his case.

We figured after McGill heard our story, he would have enough evidence for a judge to issue a search warrant for the private property along the creek. The police would eventually ID the body buried under the shack and then they would have two murders to solve.

It was turning out to be the summer of death in Albany.

The Kinchafoonee Creek in my mind was no longer a place of natural beauty, and a place where Abby and I had made love on top of a blanket near the Blue Hole. The sand was soft as was her tanned body. Now those slow, peaceful waters represented something else. Something sinister.

We decided to try to talk with McGill before going to the newsroom and updating Mickey on what had happened to us at the creek. He would want a story after the police had located the body under the shack. My guess was McGill would have his people on the creek sometime this morning.

It was seven forty-five and we were sitting in two black vinyl chairs at the APD waiting on McGill to arrive. We were drinking coffee I had bought in a machine in the courthouse. The shift was changing and cops were coming in and out of the department. We were told McGill usually arrived just a few minutes before eight.

As we waited, we reviewed our notes that we had written last night in our notepads that chronicled the day's events on the creek.

"Then I dug up a dead man who looked as if he had been shot in the head…" During my short career as a newspaper reporter, this was a sentence I had never written before last night.

We were both focused on our notes and did not hear McGill approach us.

"Good morning, Mr. Maynard," McGill said. "Y'all waiting on me or somebody else?"

"Yes, sir, Detective McGill," I said. "We'd like to see you. We've got something I think you'll want to hear."

"It's related to the Maria Rios case," Abby said. "We've got some information that will help you. We hope it will help you find who killed Maria."

"Abby Sinclair, right?" McGill said.

"Yes, that's right."

"I've seen your stories and they're good. I know who you are. You two working the case together now? The Maria Rios case?"

"That's right, we're both on it," Abby said.

"Follow me to my desk," McGill said.

We took the two chairs in front of McGill's desk. Green vinyl this time. He poured himself a cup of coffee from a pot sitting on the desk of another detective. Then he re-filled our cups.

McGill was wearing a short-sleeved white shirt and a dark-blue tie. He sat behind his desk and removed a black pen and a large yellow notepad from the top drawer.

"Usually it's the other way around," McGill said.

"Other way around?" I said. "What do you mean?"

"We're the ones usually giving out the information," McGill said. "Not you giving it to us."

"Oh, I see. I understand what you mean."

"What we have will help your investigation, Detective McGill," Abby said. "You ready?"

"Go ahead, Miss Sinclair. I'm listening."

McGill took pen in hand and began to write as Abby told him our story. As she was talking, I flipped through my notes following the timeline of events that began with the Monkey Palace and seeing Big Foot and Senator Whitfield together. She was brief with that part of it.

She included my run-in with Pearl and the fact that Skeeter and I saw him on the beach with those young girls. Young like Maria Rios. Abby's focus was on yesterday and the man I dug up.

She was thorough, and I knew she would be. She didn't refer to her notes in the telling of it. Abby spoke in a slow manner allowing McGill the opportunity to take good notes. But she only spoke for a couple of minutes.

There was nothing for me to add when she had finished. Then McGill stopped writing but kept the pen in his hand. He took a drink of coffee and so did we.

"I know the property you're talking about off Uncle Jim's Lane," McGill said. "We drove down there after we found the girl. After we found Maria Rios. Even interviewed a few of the folks who live down there. We were looking for leads and didn't find any."

"You have one now," I said. "You have one big lead."

"Yeah, looks like it," McGill said. "My first question is this, why didn't you call us last night and let us know about the body? We could've got started on this then. We would've been out there by now."

Abby and I looked at one another. I didn't have a good answer for McGill. Neither did Abby. He was right. We should've notified the police the moment we returned to my house from the creek.

"We probably should've," I said. "Just figured the body wasn't going anywhere. I guess we were shook up a little bit, too. Not thinking clear. Scared and tired. We both wrote some notes, had a glass of wine and went to bed. Haven't gone to the newsroom yet to tell our editor all of this. We thought it was more important to come here first. You're right, we should've called APD last night."

"Well, you had every right to be all scared, tired, and shook up," McGill said. "And usually they don't."

"They don't what?" Abby said.

"Usually the bodies don't go anywhere on their own," McGill said. "In all my years of policing, they don't move once they're dead. Someone has to move them."

"Oh, yeah, I guess so," Abby said. "I see what you mean."

"I got another question for you two," McGill said.

"What is it?" Abby said.

"Mr. Maynard, you positive you saw Senator Whitfield at the Monkey Palace?" McGill said. "You sure it was him you followed to the creek the next morning? You positive? You saw him with the owner of the Monkey Palace?"

"Positive it was him," I said. "I've interviewed the senator before. Covered a couple of his press conferences. I know what he looks like. I know who he is."

"Are you implying you think the senator has got something to do with Maria Rios' death?" McGill said. "Is that what I'm hearing you say?"

"No, detective," Abby said. "We are not implying that or anything else. We are just giving you information that we hope leads to the arrest of whoever killed Maria Rios. And whoever killed the man John dug up."

McGill looked over his notes and leaned back in his chair with the pen still in his hand. He took another drink of coffee.

"Is there anything else you two want to tell me?"

"That's it," Abby said. "We've covered it. You know all that we know."

"She's right," I said. "Abby covered everything we know that might help your investigation. She didn't leave anything out."

"All right, then, I appreciate your help on this," McGill said. "I should be able to get a search warrant signed this morning and have my people on the creek in the next couple of hours. Hopefully, we'll know something about the victim by the end of the day."

"We'll check back with you this afternoon for an ID of the body," Abby said.

"Fair enough," McGill said. "Give me a call after lunch sometime and I'll tell you want we have."

"Final question, Detective McGill," Abby said.

"What is it?"

"Do you have anything new on the Maria Rios case?" Abby said. "Anything we can report."

"No, Miss Sinclair, we don't. But I do have some advice for you. For both of you."

"What is it?" Abby said.

"I can see where your heart is on this case and I understand," Mc-Gill said. "It was horrific what was done to her. But you two stay away from the creek. That's my advice to you. Let us handle it from here. We're going to find out who's doing the killing out there. We'll stop it."

"I understand your concern, Detective McGill," Abby said. "But I'm going to do everything I can to find out who killed her. We've got to make sure this doesn't happen to other girls. We've got to stop the killings."

"That's what we all want."

We left McGill and headed for the newsroom. Mickey needed to hear the same story we had told the detective. Now there were two dead bodies that had been found near the Kinchafoonee Creek within days of one another. They were connected, both of us believed that.

The other thing I believed when we left the courthouse that morning was that McGill's warning was not going to keep us away from the creek. Or anywhere else involving this case. Abby was not to be deterred. And like she said, we were just doing our jobs.

CHAPTER 27

"Goddamnit, Abby, I bet Maynard will do whatever you say for the rest of his life," Mickey said. "You're one bad-ass reporter. And I thought I was tough. Hell, I'll do whatever you say now."

That was the first thing Mickey said to us after we told him about what had happened on the creek and that we had met with Detective McGill before coming to work. He was most impressed with Abby knocking the hell out of Pearl. I was too.

One of Mickey's favorite lines to all of his reporters was, "Get the facts and don't take any shit from anybody." Abby was well-trained.

"Well, all I want John to do now is to help find out who killed Maria Rios," Abby said. "Mickey, we can't let this happen to any other girls. That's what matters now. That's all that matters."

"Stay on it then," Mickey said. "But goddamnit, be careful you two. McGill's right. Stay away from the goddamn Kinchafoonee until this thing is resolved. Let the cops do their job. You report what they tell you. Got it? I can always find something else for you two to do around here until they make an arrest."

"Mickey, we'll be okay," I said. "Don't worry about us. We'll have something for tomorrow's paper from McGill. Hopefully they'll be able to ID the body by this afternoon. I'll let you know. We think the two killings are related."

"We'll run it page one," Mickey said. "But this might not have anything to do with the girl. It could be separate altogether."

"Maybe, but we think the murders are connected," Abby said. "Based on everything we know about the story, we think the killings are connected."

*

About one-thirty that afternoon I got a telephone call from Detective McGill. He asked us to come to the police department, and I figured he had some information on the body that I had dug up. I got Abby, and we headed across Pine Avenue to the courthouse. The sun was hot, the sky a hazy blue. The traffic was slow as we crossed Pine Avenue in a hurry.

McGill was at his desk looking through a tan folder when we arrived. He saw us walk toward him.

"Good to see you two again. Have a seat," McGill said.

"Were you able to identify the body?" Abby said. "Who is he and is he connected with Maria Rios?"

"How would I know?" McGill said. "There was no dead body. There was no dead body in a black bag. There was no dead man with a bullet in his head. We found nothing but dirt under that shack. That's all. Just dirt. We found the shack but not a dead man."

"Dirt?" I said. "What do you mean *dirt*? There's a body in that shack and I saw it. Abby saw it. Hell, I dug the damn thing up. You're telling us you didn't find it? Bodies don't get up and walk away, do they?"

"Yes, I'm telling you that because that's the truth," McGill said. "We did not find a body. You're right. Bodies don't walk away on their own."

"What do you mean there's no body?" Abby said. "We saw it. We smelled it. You had to find it. What do you *mean* there was no body?"

"I mean just what I said. There was *no dead man*. This is very simple and I'll say it again. There. Was. No. Body."

"It had to be there," Abby said. "Dead people don't walk. We saw it. John dug it up. I held the flashlight."

"Maybe all that's true . . ."

"Maybe? Is that what you said, Detective McGill?" Abby said.

"Miss Sinclair, I don't doubt you and your partner saw a body. I'm just telling you, there's not one there now. I can't explain to you what happened and who did what. I can only tell you that I took three officers out there by boat, dug in that shack where you said the body was and found only dirt."

"Any signs of the body being removed?" I said.

"No, nothing to indicate anything was moved," McGill said. "Just an old cabin that's been there forever. That's all we found."

"How about the smell?" Abby said. "Was there an awful smell? We smelled it, didn't we John? The death smell."

"No, didn't smell a body, and I know what one smells like," McGill said. "I promise you that. It smelled dirty, like an old cabin. No death smell."

"Did you see the witch tree statue?" I said. "We told you about that. Abby used it on Pearl. Was it there?"

"It was there," McGill said. "Hard to charge a statue with murder, especially since there's no dead body or gun."

"Detective McGill, this is not a joke," Abby said. "Two people are dead and we could've gotten killed out there. Out on the Kinchafoon-ee."

"I apologize, Miss Sinclair," McGill said. "I didn't mean to make light of a very serious situation. I know you want this case solved as much as I do. And, yes, you and Mr. Maynard could've gotten killed out there. That's why I'm asking you two to stay away from the creek."

"The body's been moved, Detective McGill," Abby said. "Whoever we heard in that vehicle moved it. They must've seen the light from my flashlight when John was digging. We ran and they took the body and buried it somewhere else. That's what happened."

"Who? Who's they?" McGill said.

"Pearl, Big Foot, hell we don't know for sure," I said. "Whoever was in that vehicle we heard in the woods. It was coming toward the cabin. They moved it. They moved the body. We told you all about Pearl and Big Foot."

"Maybe so," McGill said. "Somebody moved it because it damn sure ain't there. Look, I been doing this before you two were born. I know a dead body when I see one. And I didn't see one."

"Did you talk to anyone when you went out there?" Abby said. "Did you go up to that big house, that longhouse that we saw a few days ago? That's the place we overheard Pearl and Big Foot talking. Who did you interview?"

"We interviewed no one, Miss Sinclair. Didn't have enough evidence of a crime. Still don't have any evidence of a crime."

"How about the woman who owns the land?" Abby said. "The one married to the county commissioner in Camilla. Did you interview her?"

"The same answer. No," McGill said. "I don't make it a habit to interview citizens about a crime of which we have no evidence. Do you understand, Miss Sinclair?"

"I'm trying to understand, Detective McGill," Abby said. "We're both trying to understand. Right now it's a little difficult."

"Had we found the body, we would've interviewed the people you mentioned. Again, no dead body, no evidence of a crime. No interviews."

"What now?" I said. "What do we do now, Detective McGill?"

"You do what I said this morning," McGill said. "You let us handle it. Keep checking in with me, and I'll keep you updated about the Maria Rios case. We'll find who did it. There's just nothing this department can do about the dead man you say you saw out there last night."

"Say you saw?" Abby said. "We said it because it was the truth. You think we made this up? You think that's what this is about?"

"Oh, I don't doubt you, Miss Sinclair," McGill said. "You two aren't the kind of reporters that make up things. I know that."

"No, we don't make things up," I said. "I haven't been a reporter near as long as you been in law enforcement, but I know a dead person when I see one. Especially one that I dug up. One with a bullet hole in his head."

"Okay, okay, I'll tell you what I'm going to do," McGill said. "I'll send some of my boys back to the creek, and to the Monkey Palace if need be, to find these guys – Pearl and Big Foot. And I have a contact down at the Mitchell County Sheriff's Office who can speak with the county commissioner. The one whose wife owns the land. Does that make you feel better?"

"Us? It should make you feel better," Abby said.

"We'll see about that," McGill said. "I feel pretty good right now."

"We'll stay in touch with you," I said.

"I know you will, but let us do our job," McGill said. "I don't want you two getting hurt out there or anywhere else. We're going to figure out who killed Maria Rios and we'll make an arrest. I promise you that. And if something comes from these interviews today, we'll find that body and who put him there. Is that a deal?"

"That's a deal," I said.

"What about you, Miss Sinclair?"

"Detective McGill, I'm not worried about getting hurt," Abby said. "I'm concerned with the truth and who killed Maria Rios. I'm concerned with other girls ending up like her. And I believe the body John dug up is connected with her. That's what I believe. That's my deal."

CHAPTER 28

Back in the newsroom after meeting with McGill, we told Mickey the police didn't find the body I had dug up along the creek. There would be no story for tomorrow's paper.

He wasn't surprised. Surprises didn't exist in the newsroom.

"Those goddamn creeps on the creek are killers," Mickey said. "I don't care how hard Abby hit the guy. What's his name?"

"Pearl," I said. "They call him Pearl."

"Yeah, Pearl," Mickey said. "You still don't know his real name?"

"Not yet," I said. "We'll find out, though. Soon enough."

"Listen, you two stay away from out there for a while," Mickey said. "Let McGill and the GBI handle this. They'll figure it all out. I'll keep you busy around here with something else until this story breaks. They'll find who killed the girl. And who killed the man you dug up."

"We think whoever was in the vehicle we heard removed the body after we ran out of the shack," Abby said. "I don't see another explanation right now. John says the same thing."

"You agree with that, Maynard?" Mickey said.

"Yeah, it makes sense," I said. "They could've been in a green van or a white Blazer. Those are the two vehicles connected with this thing so far. The two that I've seen."

"You could put a body in either one of those vehicles," Mickey said. "I don't give a goddamn about the vehicles and the body right now. You two just stay away from the creek and the woods out there for now. This is South Georgia, need I remind you? People can die for all kinds of reasons in the woods. And I suppose a body can be moved from one place to another."

"But where?" Abby said. "Where would they've moved it? Would they bury it somewhere else on that property or take it away altogether?"

"Lots of places out there in the woods," I said. "It's dense. It wouldn't be hard for them to move the body, dig another hole and drop him in. Maybe they did it closer to the creek where the land is sandy and easy for digging. I saw a couple of areas like that not far from the shack."

"Goddamn you two!" Mickey said. "Do I need to say it again? Louder maybe. Stay away from the Kinchafoonee for now. Let the cops handle the leg work. That's their job."

"We will, Mickey," I said. "Just speculating. That's all."

"Abby?" Mickey said. "Are you listening? I don't have time to worry about you two and this story. Are you listening?"

"Yes, I'm listening, but John's right," Abby said. "We're just speculating. I was hoping, we were hoping, that the dead man would lead us to whoever killed Maria Rios. I'm just worried about other girls. And now other men."

"You should be, Abby, because we just learned about two missing girls from down in Brooks County," Mickey said. "The story just broke. Charlie Moon is on it, he's got good sources down there…"

Abby said nothing to Mickey as she turned away from his desk, as a determined mother would move to help an injured child, and walked to where Charlie Moon was sitting at his desk typing the story of the two missing girls from Brooks County. I stayed and looked at Mickey.

"Well, go ahead and go talk to Charlie," Mickey said. "I know you want to. It's obvious she does. Find out what he has. Go."

"Okay, I do want to hear what he's got."

I followed Abby to Charlie's desk.

Charlie was in his early forties and had been a reporter for the *Chronicle* for about fifteen years. Before joining the newspaper he had worked for a couple of weeklies, one in Bainbridge and the other in Cairo, both south of Albany. All he ever wanted since he was fifteen was to write stories for newspapers.

He got his love of reading and writing from his mother, who taught high school English in Thomasville, about fifty miles south of Albany.

To Charlie, working for a newspaper was not actual *work*. It wasn't a job. It was joy.

"Shit, Maynard, where in the hell else in this crazy-ass world are you goin' to ride around the countryside, talk to people, write stories and get a pay check?" Charlie said to me the first time I met him. "That ain't work. That's stealin' money without consequences. I ain't nothin' but a thief who writes stories and people read them. And people know me. Some love me and others want to cut my heart out and feed it to the hogs. "

He said it to me more than once and each time he laughed hard and long, usually slapping my back. He was a great storyteller and always fun to be around. I learned something about writing and reporting every time I was around him.

Charlie Moon still lived in Thomasville. He wrote stories in his home office and telephoned them to the *Chronicle*. He covered several counties south of Albany, including Brooks. It was rare he was in the newsroom two out of five days. He stayed on the move in his territory. He liked it that way.

A few years earlier, Charlie made national news after winning Associated Press Awards for a series of stories involving the killing of a farm-family in Donaldsonville, Georgia. Eight members of the Alton family were murdered by three escaped convicts from Reidsville State Prison in Georgia.

The three killers were Georgia boys, all in their twenties, who had been sent to prison for armed robbery, rape, and killing two cops in Macon. All in one night.

The killers tortured three members of the Alton family before they died and one was an eighty-one year old woman. Charlie's reporting and writing were both stellar, earning him the recognition from the AP. He was one of the best reporters in the Southeast. He wrote features and hard news and knew the underbelly of South Georgia better than any reporter in the state. He had seen a lot of ugliness.

Everywhere you went in South Georgia, people knew Charlie Moon and his work for the *Chronicle*. As he told me, some hated him, others loved him. The ones who hated him, hated the truth. Charlie was a bulldog in pursuit of the truth. He knew every lawman from Albany to the Florida border. The ones that liked him, he often drank bourbon with. Sometimes during the work day.

"There's truth in wine, Maynard," Charlie said. "Never forget that. When you want the truth form a source, wine can take you there. It works nearly all the time."

Charlie never drank wine. But he'd buy his sources whatever they preferred. He preferred cheap bourbon over three cubes of ice. Just three. If he didn't have any ice, he'd drank it anyway. Sometimes in his coffee when he was writing.

"Charlie, can we talk to you for a minute?" Abby said. "I know you're working on a story for tomorrow but it'll only take a minute."

Charlie stopped typing and looked at Abby. He was wearing a tie-less long-sleeved white shirt with the sleeves rolled to his elbows. He was about five ten, but two hundred and thirty-five pounds. His thick black hair needed to be combed. It always did. Charlie was good at writing but not so good at other things, like personal hygiene.

"Sure, Abby, anytime," Charlie said. "I always got time for the paper's prettiest reporter and our smartest one, too. I ain't talkin' 'bout you, Maynard."

"No, shit, Charlie," I said. "I know who you're talking about."

Charlie was chain smoking Marlboros and said he was trying to cut back to a pack a day instead of the two-and-a-half he had built up to. He and Mickey were about even on that. Said he was trying to lose weight, too. But he never tried hard to do either one of those things. He drank black coffee that was probably cold. He could stretch a cup out for an hour or more, especially if he was adding bourbon to it. I detected no signs of liquor.

"What can you tell us about the two missing girls?" Abby said. "Mickey told us you're working on the story out of Brooks County. Can you tell us about it?"

"Sure, you two have a seat," Charlie said.

We sat in two chairs next to Charlie's desk. Abby had gotten her notepad and a pen. She started to write when Charlie started talking.

Charlie said they were both fifteen and had been born in Honduras. They had been working on separate farms in Brooks County, not far from Charlie's Thomasville home, and were reported missing today. Their names were Ana Flores and Gabriella Molina. Charlie had received a call from one of his sources in the Brooks County Sheriff's Office. Brooks was not far from Mitchell County where Maria Rios was taken.

The girls were not related but had arrived in Georgia about the same time about three months ago. Charlie was planning to make additional calls to Brooks County later that evening before filing his story. He gave us all the information he had, but as of now it was limited.

"Have you contacted Detective McGill with the Albany Police Department?" Abby said. "You think they're connected with Maria Rios? You think the same people who killed her kidnapped these girls in Brooks? What did McGill say about that?"

"Haven't called him yet," Charlie said. "I'm trying to get the first part of the story down and then I'll call over there and see if I can get a quote or two from him. Mickey told me you two have been following the girl's story. Said you got yourselves in some shit. Some real shit. He didn't give me all the details. Just said he was worried about you. I don't know if these things are connected, but if you make me guess, I'd say yes."

"Charlie, you think they're going to kill the two girls that were kidnapped today?" Abby said.

"I'm not saying that," Charlie said. "Young, pretty girls are being kidnapped not to be killed. They're to be used for something else. You understand? And it's not working in the fields picking vegetables."

"So what about Maria Rios?" Abby said. "Why did she end up tortured and killed?"

"Whoever did that to her, that wasn't in the plan," Charlie said. "That got out of control. Someone lost their mind or minds with that girl. Like I said, whoever is doing this ain't doing it to kill girls. Bad enough snatching young girls away from their families, but what happened to that little girl off Palmyra Road was pure evil. There's goddamn evil out there, Abby. Southern hospitality, my ass. Pure evil."

"That's what we're trying to stop," Abby said. "We're trying to stop the evil."

"How long had those two girls been in Georgia?" I said. "Were you able to find that out?"

"Like I said, according to my sources both of the families got here about three months ago," Charlies said. "Same story. Good folks trying to get away from bad things happening in their country. Violent place Honduras. People cut your head off for a bag of cocaine. And then give the severed head to your mother. They come here for a better life but, goddamnit, it doesn't always work out like that."

"No, it doesn't," Abby said.

"Are they getting close to an arrest on your case?" Charlie said. "The girl they found off Palmyra. What's McGill saying?"

"If they are, they haven't told us," I said. "We did have a few new developments yesterday. I think Mickey told you about that."

"Yeah, but he didn't give me many details," Charlie said. "Tell me what happened. I want to hear it all."

I told Charlie about the dead body I dug up and that the police didn't find it when they searched the shack. And I told him everything we had seen and heard involving Pearl, Big Foot, Skeeter, and Senator Whitfield. Even told him about Abby using the witch tree statue to knock out Pearl.

"That Whitfield is a real dickhead," Charlie said. "I've known him since he was twenty. He's always been a prick. Thinks he's been blessed by God Almighty. Superior to everybody else. He'd steal a quarter off your dead grandmother. I swear he would. He's a prickhead. Ain't capable of violence. I don't think so anyway."

"Charlie, will you do us favor?" Abby said.

"No, not until you tell me one thing."

"What's that?"

"How did it feel to knock the hell out of that redneck? The one in the shack. What was his name? Pearl?"

"Yeah, Pearl. And it felt pretty good after John told me I didn't kill him," Abby said.

"It takes a lot to kill a creek-running, liquor-drinking redneck," Charlie said. "I know. I've seen many of them. Now tell me what I can do for you two?"

"Just let us know about any developments with those two girls today, that's all," Abby said. "We all need to do what we can to get them back to their families. God help them."

"Whatever I find out, I'll tell you and John," Charlie said. "You two do the same. I've got some good sources down there. Had them for years. They'll shoot straight with me. I buy them a good bottle of bourbon every month or so. I get what I want."

"Thanks, Charlie. Thanks a lot," Abby said.

"There's evil out there," Charlie said. "Y'all be careful. Real careful. But in the meantime, don't take any shit from a half-ass redneck."

"Oh, Charlie, she won't," I said. "You should've seen her in action yesterday. She knocked the shit out of that good-ole-boy."

"I call that just good reporting," Charlie said. "But still be careful. I'd be a little scared if I was you two. Might want to stay away from the Kinchafoonee for a while. Sounds like that Pearl fellow is capable doing some mean shit."

"Charlie, we aren't near as sacred as Maria Rios was when she was taken and tortured," Abby said. "Or those two girls you're writing about now from Brooks County. They're scared, Charlie. If they're still alive. I can't imagine how they felt."

"You're right, Abby. Of course you are," Charlie said. "Just be careful. That's all I'm saying. There's evil out there. Pure, pure evil."

CHAPTER 29

Around four-thirty we said goodbye to Charlie Moon and left for the Monkey Palace. I sure as hell didn't want to see Pearl again. Even in a public place, he could be unpredictable. He had proven that.

Abby had other plans. She was intent on us trying to talk with the bartender, Sugar Baby, in efforts to pull any information out of him that would help us understand the relationship among Pearl, Big Foot, and Senator Whitfield.

She wanted anything that might lead us to who killed Maria Rios, the man I dug up, and now, who kidnapped the two young girls from Honduras who were working in Brooks County. Evil is a strong word, but it applied to this story.

I drove us to the Monkey Palace, but I was hoping to change her mind on the way. If Pearl was there, he might try to kill us. She promised me that if we walked in and saw Pearl, we would leave in a hurry. Run if we had to.

"I think we need to talk with the bartender," Abby said. "He was easy to talk to. We may get something out of him. What's his name? Sugar Man? Sugar Dude?"

"His name is *Sugar Baby*. I don't like this idea right now. We can stay if we don't see Pearl. But we ain't staying long. Understand? Remember what Mickey told us?"

"Yes, I remember what Mickey said. He said stay away from the creek for a while. We're not going near the creek, John. We're going to have a drink at the Monkey Palace and talk for a minute or two. That's all."

"Great idea, Abby. Maybe we'll see Pearl and he'll buy us a drink and sit with us. Talk about all the good times we've had together. I can't wait."

"John, don't worry about Pearl cutting off your balls. I know how to take care of him."

"Oh, now my baby has been transformed into an ass-kickin' reporter just like Mickey said. Who would have thought such a thing? Not me, that's for sure."

"People change, John. That's what life is all about. Didn't your parents ever explain that to you?"

"I'm sure they did, I just don't remember right now. But I do know one thing for sure, Abby."

"What's that?"

"Pearl would like to beat the shit out of both of us now. I think you'd get it worse than I would. His head is probably still the size of a basketball."

"His head was already big. I told you not to worry about him. I'm sure I can find something in the Monkey Palace to hit him with."

"Is that supposed to be funny? Do you see me laughing? You know you're really starting to be a hard-ass about this. Damn stubborn."

"What are you going to say next, John? That a woman should stay in her place. That a woman should always follow her man's lead. What's next, partner?"

"I'm not going to say any of that. You know better. First of all, I don't believe those things. Second, I don't want you to do to me what you did to Pearl."

"Charlie Moon said I was the smartest reporter at the *Chronicle*," Abby said. "Now I'm beginning to think it may be you."

Abby leaned over in the front seat of my car, put her left arm around my neck and kissed me several times on my cheek and neck. The kisses were slow. She knew how to get to me.

We pulled into the Monkey Palace parking lot. I turned to give her my full attention. We kissed long and deep. That taste knocked me off balance.

"Is there any more of that available for later?" I said.

"Are you saying you want to make love with a woman that would hit a man on his head? Hit him hard, too."

"That's exactly what I'm saying."

"Of course there's always more available for you, Johnny Boy. As long as you remember what Charlie Moon said about me."

"I knew that long before Charlie did."

"You keep talking like that and you'll get what you want. I promise you."

*

Inside the Monkey Palace the crowd was light, but that would change as the evening moved on. Sugar Baby was at his usual place, behind the bar mixing drinks, smiling, and making his customers laugh. He was good at it.

There were several seats available at the bar, and we sat down with the sounds of Earth, Wind & Fire on eight track. The music was not loud and you didn't have to strain to talk over it. There were a handful of couples dancing and one in a corner deep kissing.

All six of the monkeys were awake and seemed to be taking careful notice of those looking at them. A few moments after we sat at the bar, Sugar Baby approached us.

"All right, John and Abby! Albany's finest reporters," Sugar Baby said. "Always good to see you two again. What can I get you?"

"I'll take a Bud," I said.

"A glass of white wine for me, Sugar Baby," Abby said.

"Comin' right up," Sugar Baby said.

A minute later, the beer and wine were in front of us sitting on coasters imprinted with a large monkey with a drink in his hand. A few others sat at the bar, and I figured we had some time to talk to Sugar Baby before the place got busy. Our questions wouldn't take long.

I looked all around the bar and didn't see Pearl. Didn't see Big Foot, either. Then I took a long drink of beer before I asked the first question.

"Got a question for you, Sugar Baby," I said.

"Like I said before, I get a lot of 'em. Ask away."

"Is Big Foot coming in tonight? I'd like to talk to him if I could."

"Now that's a question I ain't got a good answer for."

"What do you mean?" Abby said.

"He went fishing a few days ago and was supposed to be back by now. He ain't called either. He'll show up soon. I just don't know when. He went in one hole and I suppose he'll come out another. Just like a raccoon in the woods."

"Where'd he go fishing?" I said.

Big Foot, according to Sugar Baby, had gone to Panama City Beach, Florida, and chartered a deep-sea fishing boat out of Captain Anderson's fleet. He was after red snapper and grouper. It was supposed to be a three-night trip. Big Foot was supposed to have been back to work yesterday, but he wasn't.

"Who did he go with?" Abby said.

"He didn't say and I didn't ask," Sugar Baby said. "I never ask. He's got a lot of friends. None of my business anyway. Man, there's lots of things down there he likes. Lots of girls and liquor. Lots of dancin' girls at Miss Newby's. All they're wearin' is little more than what the Good Lord gave 'em. Big Foot does like his fun."

"You worried about him?" I said.

"*Worried*. Hell no, I ain't worried," Sugar Baby said. "He's a big boy. Why should I worry? He knows his limits. Most of the time. He may show up here late tonight. Wouldn't be surprised."

"He's probably having a big time down there," I said. "It's easy to do in Panama City."

"Why did you need to see him?" Sugar Baby said. "If he calls tonight, I can tell 'im you two were looking for 'im."

"That's okay, Sugar Baby," Abby said. "It can wait until he gets back. Our editor has us working on a series of stories about unique Albany businesses. We wanted to include the Monkey Palace."

I took a drink of beer, looked at Abby and smiled. Damn, she's quick, I thought. Just one of the many reasons I was in love with her.

"That's right, Sugar Baby," I said. "It was Abby's idea to include the Palace. Our editor liked it, too. We love this place. A lot of people do. We'll talk to Big Foot when he gets back. No problem."

"Man, you're *so* right," Sugar Baby said. "Ain't nothin' else like this in Albany. Probably the whole damn state. Big Foot will like that. As soon as he gets back, I'll tell 'im."

"Another question for you Sugar Baby," Abby said.

"You reporters just can't help yourselves, can you?"

"Not her, Sugar Baby. Not Abby."

"What is it this time?" Sugar Baby said.

"You think Pearl went fishing with Big Foot?" Abby said. "John would sure hate to see Pearl in here tonight. They didn't get along too well at the bar the last time. Did they?"

"Oh, yeah, I do remember those two *not* getting along so well," Sugar Baby said. "Pearl sure knows how to make friends."

"You think he went fishing with Big Foot?" I said.

"Could've. But I don't know who went with im," Sugar Baby said. "Pearl and Big Foot, they do spend some time together. Drinkin' and fishin' mostly. They could be together on this trip. Hadn't seen Pearl in a few days, either."

"Final question, Sugar Baby," I said.

"I don't believe it, but go ahead."

"How about Senator Whitfield?" I said. "Has he come in the last few days? Have you seen him?"

"That's another *no*. I think I saw 'im on TV a day or two ago. He ain't been in here since Big Foot left."

"You'd probably know when a United States senator comes into your place for a drink, wouldn't you?" Abby said.

"Sure as collard greens are green. Sure as white on rice. Nothin' happens here without me knowin' it. That's why Big Foot hired me. Every penny is where it should be every night. Ain't nothin' happenin' here without Sugar Baby knowin' it. You can take that shit to the bank and deposit it."

"We believe you, Sugar Baby," Abby said. "We believe you. We know how things work here."

"We just appreciate you talking with us," I said. "Always do."

"I do that every day and every night," Sugar Baby said. "Glad to do it with you two. Anytime and every time."

*

I bought a bottle of Merlot for us on the way to my house and stopped at the Villa Gargano along Slappey Boulevard, Abby's favorite restaurant, where I picked up a large pepperoni pizza. The best in Albany and the best in the South.

At home I opened the wine and played a Carole King album, *Tapestry*, another one of Abby's favorites. We sat on the sofa and had pizza and wine. I had some plans of my own for the evening, and they didn't include Big Foot or Pearl.

I hadn't forgotten what Abby said in the Monkey Palace parking lot after our slow kiss. But her thoughts were still focused on the story. There's "evil" out there Charlie Moon said. Abby had her mind on it.

"You know what I'm thinking, John?" Abby said. "Do you?"

"I hope it's the same thing I'm thinking. I'm thinking about that kiss this afternoon in the parking lot. It was like a well-written lede. Something good to build on. Don't you think?"

"We got all night, John. I'm thinking about something else right now. I'm thinking about this story we're on."

"Of course you are. Okay, I'll play along. What are you thinking exactly? I bet I can guess. You can't stop thinking about this . . ."

"Was the body in the bag Big Foot? You think he was killed by Pearl? Did it look like Big Foot? Could you tell?"

"Shit, Abby, you saw what I saw. We saw the back of a man's head with a hole in it. Lots of dried, purple blood. Black and blue everywhere. I couldn't even tell you what color of hair he had. Or if he had any. I'm pretty sure we saw a dead man and not a dead woman. That's about all I can say. How long do you think we got a look at him? Two seconds or three? How could anybody tell who it was?"

"I know, I know, John. I sure couldn't tell for certain, either. But think about what Sugar Baby said. Big Foot has been gone longer than he said he would be. He hasn't called the Monkey Palace. Does that seem normal for somebody who runs a business?"

"That means he's dead? That means Pearl or somebody else killed him and buried him under the shack? What's the motive? Hell, he's probably drinking all day at the No-Name Bar in Panama City and going to Miss Newby's strip club at night."

"Something you've done?"

"I'm not saying either way. Better yet, no comment. Let's talk about the story we're on. I don't want you to hit me over the head with this heavy lamp. I've seen what you can do."

"I would never do that to you, Johnny Boy. Unless you deserved it, never forget that. I'm just trying to make some sense of what Sugar Baby told us."

"How? He told us Big Foot went fishing, he hadn't seen Pearl or the senator for a few days. Now you think you know who was buried underneath that shack on the creek? I think you need to slow down a bit."

"Don't tell me to slow down, *John*. There was a dead man buried out there, and I bet it's somebody we've seen in the Monkey Palace and on the Kinchafoonee."

"Maybe. Maybe not. It could be someone we've never seen before. Someone who's never been in the Monkey Palace. The only thing we know for sure is that we don't know who it is."

I poured more wine in our glasses and flipped the Carole King album to the other side. I moved closer to Abby on the sofa. Then the phone rang. I thought about not answering it because of what was on my mind. But I did it anyway.

"Maynard, this is Charlie Moon. We need to talk. I got something you and Abby need to know."

"What do you got, Charlie?"

"The FBI has been watching some of those characters on the Kinchafoonee. The same ones you and Abby are watching."

"What's the story?"

"Child sex-ring with possible connections in Central America. My source won't go on the record and says the FBI office out of Atlanta won't either at this point. I trust the guy. He's been reliable over the years."

"Are they close to making any arrests?" I said.

"I asked him that question, and he said he just doesn't know enough to answer either way. He's not directly connected with the investigation."

"What do we do now, Charlie?"

"Stay on the story but, goddamnit, be careful. I'm going to stay on my sources in Brooks County about the two missing girls. I just wanted you and Abby to know what my source said. Hopefully this thing will be over soon. The feds are usually pretty good at what they do."

"Did you tell Mickey?" I said.

"Not yet. I wanted you and Abby to know as soon as possible. I'll call him first thing in the morning. I'm going to be on the road tomorrow. You can tell him the same thing if you want."

"Okay, Charlie. Anything else we need to know?"

"You know what I know now. Just be smart out there. There's some real assholes runnin' around. It's South Georgia. Like I said, southern hospitality."

"Thanks, Charlie."

I took a long drink of wine and moved even closer to Abby, putting my right arm around here, drawing her close to me.

"It was Charlie Moon, wasn't it?" Abby said. "What did he say? What did he say about the girls? Have there been arrests made?"

"Not yet. No arrest. Said he talked to a source today who told him the FBI was investigating a possible child sex-ring involving that group on the Kinchafoonee. Pearl and Big Foot."

"Was or is?" Abby said.

"What do you mean?"

"John, is the investigation over or is it continuing? Which is it?"

"It's ongoing, Charlie said."

"When are they going to make the arrests? What did he say about that?"

"He said his source didn't know," I said. "Said his source only knew that an investigation was underway. And that if you asked the FBI about it at this point, they would deny it. They must not have enough evidence to make an arrest."

"John, we got to tell the FBI about the body. Did Charlie tell them?"

"He didn't say either way."

"We need to contact the FBI and tell them," Abby said. "It may push them along on their investigation."

"There is no body, remember? McGill took a team out there and didn't find a body."

"I don't give a damn about that," Abby said. "You know there was a body and I do too. We need to contact the FBI."

"Maybe. Let's think about. We just got to figure out our next move."

"Our next move?"

"That's what I said, Abby."

"To help those girls, John. That's our next move."

"You know what, Abby?"

"What?"

"Jesus, I love you."

I got up from the sofa, turned the record player off, and took Abby's hand and led her to my bedroom. I wanted both of us to try to forget this damn story for the rest of the night.

CHAPTER 30

Abby kept her promise to me. We moved beyond the telephone call from Charlie Moon, the violent story we were on, and paid attention to one another. Maybe it was Carole King and *Tapestry* that provided the inspiration I was hoping for.

Abby loved words, well spoken, well written, and well sung. I knew that the day Mickey hired her, the day we met.

I needed her. I needed her touches, her kisses, and her body pressed naked against mine. For a couple of hours that's what I got. That's what we got. I wanted her to want the same thing, and she did.

When the first beams of sunlight filtered in my bedroom the next morning, she lay naked next to me under a thin white sheet. I looked at her for a few moments in the morning light. Then I made coffee and took her a cup. A little cream and two cubes of sugar.

"It was good to forget about work for a while and focus on each other," I said. "Don't you agree? You seemed to agree last night."

"Yes, I agree. I'm sure you could tell. You're still my *very*. I love you very much."

"Not your Double Sweet?"

"That too."

"I must have been a little good to you, you never once hit me in the head with my reading lamp."

"There's no expiration date on that, is there?" Abby said. "Be careful, my love."

"Oh, I will. I've seen you in action."

"I would never have broken the lamp over your head, John. Then you wouldn't be able to read in bed."

"Read in bed? Not when I'm in bed with you."

"There you go again, saying the right thing. But you know how I feel about reading."

"Anything for you, my *very*," I said. "My Double Sweet."

"Anything? Did you say anything?"

"Oh, shit. I take it back. I take it *way* back."

"Too late, John. I need – we need – for you to call your friend Warren Crews again. We need to use his boat today. We've got to get back on the creek and to those woods again. We've got to."

"Abby! No, we don't. We can't do that. I'm not going to do that. We're not going back up there. Remember what Mickey said?"

"He said stay away for a while. It's been a while. We've got to go back up there. We've got to go this morning. Go now."

"What the hell for! What's our plan? What's your plan?"

"I want to go back to the shack and walk around in that area. I want us to look for anything, I mean anything that might help us figure out where the body has been taken. Right now the key is the body, John. That's our only evidence, and it's missing. We find out who killed that man, that's when we find out who killed Maria Rios and who kidnapped those girls from Brooks County. You understand?"

"Shit, yeah, I understand you. And you may be right. But I'm not calling Warren. We're not going back up the Kinchafoonee today. We're going to do what Mickey told us to do."

"Maybe you're not going back there today, but I am. I don't care if I have to swim, I'm going back there to see if I can find anything that will end this. I can't sit around here and wait for something else to happen. Something awful again. For another girl to be taken away from her family and tortured and killed. Call me stubborn if you want. I don't really care what you call me. It's the only thing I can think to do. Please call him."

"*Sonofabitch!*"

Warren answered his telephone after the third ring. He was getting ready to go to Albany Junior College and teach a nine o'clock American Literature class. He usually taught a couple of classes over the summer to pick up extra money for his annual August pilgrimage to Key West.

He'd spend five nights down there with a couple of his buddies fishing and drinking and walking the sacred ground of Ernest Hemingway. Five nights could mean five different girls for Warren. That was usually one of his goals anyway.

"Maynard, like I told you, you can use that boat anytime you need to. Anytime, good buddy. You don't have to ask."

"Thanks, Warren. We won't keep it long. Just need to make one more quick trip on the creek. We'll be back before your class is over."

"Don't make a difference to me. I got to teach this morning and read essays afterwards. Do what you gotta do. Have at it."

"Thanks again. This will be the last time I'll ask. Hopefully. This story we're on is about to come to end. I hope."

"All things do eventually come to an end. Just ask my three ex-wives."

"No thanks, Warren. I'll leave that subject alone."

"Smart move, my man."

After speaking with Warren, I told Abby we should check in with Mickey and maybe even make an appearance in the newsroom before heading to the creek. Mickey needed to know what the FBI had told Charlie Moon about a possible child sex-ring operation along the Kinchafoonee. If Charlie hadn't told him, we needed to.

Abby agreed that Mickey needed to know the information Charlie gave us and that Charlie would likely tell him himself. Her mind was locked again on our next move.

"We're not going to the office yet and there's no need to call Mickey," Abby said. "Let's get to the creek, we won't be there long and if Mickey gets nosey with us, we'll work it out."

"Work it out? What the hell does that mean?"

"I don't know yet," Abby said. "Stop worrying about Mickey. If he was one of us, he'd be doing the same thing we're doing."

"You're probably right," I said. "But he's not one of us, he's our boss. He'll be pissed when he finds out. Real pissed. There'll be some loud profanity. He's been very clear about all of this. He doesn't want us back on the creek."

"I've been *clear* too. Let's go."

*

Getting to Warren's boat in the daylight was easy. We didn't take a flashlight or shovel, as we did the first time. The rosebushes in his backyard still had a wonderful aroma. I breathed deep when I walked by them. Even stopped for a few seconds next to them.

I told Abby we would stay no more than fifteen minutes once we got to the shack. And to be ready to run if necessary. Our plan was to walk the area around the shack looking for anything that might explain where the body had been moved.

I thought we had little chance of finding anything helpful and a good chance of getting hurt or worse. I told Abby this more than once on the way to Warren's. She didn't give a damn.

We left Warren's dock in his johnboat about nine-thirty and headed toward the deer trail that led to the shack where I had uncovered the body that was now no longer there, according to McGill. The creek was slow. You had to look hard to see it moving.

The sun was already hot as we saw a couple of other gray-metal johnboats and morning fishermen. They waved and we did the same. They were smiling and seemed to be having fun. I was looking for Pearl but didn't see him. The yellow ball was rising in the sky.

"Going to be a hot day today, Johnny Boy. Can't wait for the fall, can you?"

"Trying to take my mind of what the hell we're doing? I know your ways. You're tricky. Very tricky."

"I'm just talking about the weather, that's all. Besides, you like some of my tricks."

"Okay, I'll play along," I said. "I'll tell you how hot it is."

"Okay, tell me. I'm listening."

"It's hotter than two buck naked rednecks – let's say their names are LeRoy and LeAnn – drinking hot sauce and screwing in a pepper patch in the middle of a July afternoon in South Georgia," I said. "How about that?"

"Oh, Johnny Boy, that's so romantic. Who said those lines? Was it Dylan Thomas or Bob Dylan?"

"It's either Richard Nixon or Richard Pryor. I can't remember exactly."

"Could you be quiet, enjoy the creek, and just drive the boat."

"Hell, no, I don't like doing this so I'm going to say any damn thing I want to."

"Well, all right. If that's how you feel, I'll let you."

"Let me! Bullshit!"

"Just kidding, John. Just kidding. Say anything you want to say if it makes you feel better."

"That's right, I will. Any damn thing I want to."

"I love it when you are a little angry and speaking in redneck-poetry," Abby said. "I just love that side of you."

"Can you just be quiet for a while?"

"No."

"Figured that."

A few minutes later our boat ride ended. What came next was becoming routine. For the third time in the last few days, we pulled a johnboat out of the Kinchafoonee Creek and hid it behind tall weeds near the deer trail that Skeeter had shown us, the one that led to the witch tree shack.

I used to come to the creek to swim, drink beer, and make love with Abby. Now I dug up dead men. Things had changed.

Our walk up the trail was more like a jog. We didn't say anything. We knew where we were going. Insect songs marked the path. We saw three deer, one large female and two white-spotted fawns, coming toward us on the trail. When they saw us, they darted off the trail and out of sight into the woods. They were probably headed to the creek for a drink, I thought.

"Much rather see deer than water moccasins, wouldn't you?" I said.

"Much rather."

We slowed when we saw the other end of the trail. The clearing was up ahead and we walked to it. Now the shack was in view. Unlike the other times we had been there, the door of the shack was wide open. Maybe whoever took the body was in too big of a hurry to close it. We stopped as we looked at the old cabin.

"That's not the way we left it, is it?" I said.

"No, that's how McGill and his team left it. Or maybe somebody after McGill."

"That's right. The cops were the last ones here. I had forgotten just for a second. I was thinking we were the last ones here. My mom always taught me to close the door when I leave the house."

"As far as we know the cops were the last ones here," Abby said. "Could've been others after the cops. We don't know for sure. We came before McGill. Remember?"

"You making fun of me?" I said.

"No, I'd never do that. Just trying to set the record straight."

Abby smiled, squeezed my right hand, and then turned it lose.

"Sometimes it's easy to forget the obvious," I said. "Especially when you're doing what we're doing. Something that could get us killed. You understand that, don't you?"

"Yes, I do. But we're doing the right thing by being here. Let's take a look inside before we walk around the area. We won't be here long. I promise."

"Remember, just a few minutes and we're out of here."

We started walking toward the shack and when we were about a hundred-and-fifty feet from it, we began to smell something horrible. It was similar to yesterday's smell at the shack. But worse. Another twenty feet and it was unbearable. The sickening smell was gagging us.

"Let's get the hell out of here, Abby. This smells going to kill us both. We'll be as dead as the man we saw here yesterday."

"No, we can't. That body must still be in there. We have to be sure. We have to see it. Cover your mouth and breathe out your nose."

"Shit, Abby, I guess you will just get us killed one way or the other."

"Just do what I do and follow me."

She covered her mouth with her right hand and I covered mine. We began our walk again to the shack, but after a few steps we stopped when something large and loud flew just a few feet over our heads.

"What the hell is that!" I said.

I said it more in a scream than a conversational tone. A moment later we knew what *that* was.

Two big, black buzzards had appeared like discreet fighter planes on the attack. They flew into the shack and out of sight. Buzzards were sometimes referred to as the Georgia Highway Eating Crew. It didn't matter to them. Rattlesnakes, rabbits, squirrels, deer, turtle, and possum, all were on the menu if they were dead on the road. They provided a public service in South Georgia.

I looked at Abby, and she pointed to the shack and from where the smell of rotting death was emanating. We got closer to the shack. Then a buzzard came out of it, looked at us and flew away with something in its mouth.

I couldn't tell for sure, but it looked like part of a hand with two or three fingers. The buzzard wasn't sharing that meal with others from the road crew.

We went inside the shack with our mouths still covered with our hands. There were about a dozen buzzards, as black as the blackest South Georgia night, eating from what appeared to be the body in the black bag I had dug up yesterday. Blackness was everywhere. I held my breath so as not to smell the awfulness of it all. I could see Abby did the same.

The body had not been moved as Detective McGill had said. Unless this was another one.

"We've got see what we can see, John. We've got to."

We walked closer to the body, and the birds moved in a way in which we could see more of it. The head and torso were fully exposed from the bag. The eyes and ears had been eaten from the head. Both cheeks had been eaten away to the bone. And the skin that was once the chin was no longer there.

The heart and lungs were almost fully exposed, and one buzzard had in its mouth what appeared to be about three feet of the victim's colon. I was about to throw up in the shack. Instead, I ran outside and vomited the bowl of Cheerios and jelly toast I had eaten before leaving my house that morning.

Abby followed me out of the cabin, put her hand on my back and when the vomiting ended, we ran from the cabin. We got to the deer trail and fast-walked to the creek without talking.

When we reached Warren's hidden boat, I counted six buzzards circling above the creek.

We pulled the boat into the water, and I ran it as fast as it would go all the way back to Warren's. From his dock, we could still see the buzzards circling.

CHAPTER 31

I parked the boat and walked past the red rosebushes to a green hose that was connected to Warren's house. The Cheerios vomit-taste in my mouth was still there. The last time I threw up was because of too many beers at a keg party a few years earlier. At least I had some fun that night.

After a thorough rinsing, I drank a belly full of water and stood next to the rosebushes breathing in deep and trying to forget the awful smell of the rotting dead man. I wanted to forget the smell and the sight of it all. But I knew no matter how long I lived, I wouldn't be able to.

"John, are you better now? The water make you feel a little better?"

"Yeah, some. At least I got that shitty taste out of my mouth. I didn't expect to do what I did."

"We didn't expect to see what we did, either," Abby said.

"How are you? Better than me, I guess. At least you didn't lose your breakfast like I did."

"It was close, though. I thought I was going to at one point. Can you hand me the hose?"

I gave Abby the hose and she drank deep from the water. She returned it to me, and I drank some more and turned the water off.

"Stand by the roses for a few minutes and breathe deep," I said. "Maybe it'll help clear our breathing. Can't hurt."

"We need a little beauty right now. They are pretty roses. You want me to drive us back to town?"

"No, I'm okay. I got us. Let's get the hell out of here."

Abby took one of my notepads and pens from the glove compartment and made notes of what we had seen that morning. She spent several minutes on it and did not talk until we were a couple of blocks from the newsroom. We parked and went inside.

We arrived at the newsroom at ten forty-five. Almost three hours late. Mickey was talking and laughing with a couple of reporters. He saw us walk in and pointed to his desk. We went straight there. We sat in front of his desk and spoke before he did.

"There's good reason we're late," I said. "You need to hear what we saw this morning."

"It better be good," Mickey said. "Because one of you could've called me. I've told you about that shit in the past. I always need to know where you are. What do you have?"

"I'll tell him, John."

I looked at Abby and nodded my head. She had the notepad on her lap. She covered the whole morning, in all of its ugly details, in a couple of minutes. When she was through, Mickey knew everything we did and saw along the Kinchafoonee Creek that morning. She didn't waste words. Her delivery was fluid and succinct.

"Maynard, did Abby leave anything out?"

"Only the part about me throwing up my breakfast after I saw the buzzards all around the body. Saw the buzzards eating away. God, that was sick. I was sick."

"What did you have for breakfast?" Mickey said.

"Cheerios and toast."

"Shit, Maynard. At least it wasn't T-Bone steak and good bourbon. I saw a lot mutilated bodies in Vietnam. The first one I saw, I threw up too. After that, it got easier. Never threw up again. Saw hundreds of bodies. Sometimes stacked up like little hills. You can get used to it."

Mickey was a Green Beret in Vietnam and often told us war stories that involved him killing the Viet Cong. Behind his desk, he kept pictures from the war and knives he had used in battle. He was cocky and tough in the newsroom, and it was easy to imagine him that way in the military. He returned from Vietnam to work at the *Chronicle*, which his father had bought when Mickey was a boy.

"I don't want to get used to it, Mickey," I said. "I don't ever want to get used to it."

"I don't either, Mickey," Abby said. "One dead, rotting body is enough for a lifetime for me."

"Here's what I'm not used to," Mickey said. "I'm not used to you two doing something I asked you not to do, goddamnit. That's what I'm not used to. I *told* you two to stay away from that creek. Don't you remember, goddamnit? Or am I losing my mind and can't remember what I say to my reporters? Is that what it is, Maynard? Abby? Maybe I'm just bat-shit crazy."

"No, Mickey, you're not losing your mind," I said. "That's what you told us. You said stay away from the creek."

"I thought so. You two are going to end up like that dead man if you're not careful. Then I won't have you around to chew your asses out. And I like chewing your asses out."

"We understand, Mickey. We do," Abby said.

There was a pause of several seconds in the conversation. No, not a conversation, an ass-chewing from Mickey.

"Abby said if you were us, you would've done the same thing this morning," I said.

"Well, well, Maynard. Goddamnit, that's beside the point. I told you two to do one thing and you did the opposite. And that *pisses* me off. You know that pisses me off."

There was another pause in the ass-chewing. It was longer this time.

"Mickey, what do you think we ought to do now?" Abby said. "McGill told us he went out there with some other cops and they didn't see the body. There's a body in the same place. John and I have seen it twice. What's are next move on this?"

Mickey lit a cigarette and took a pull, and then he blew a cloud of smoke over his head. He squinted as if he was having difficulty seeing what was before him. I didn't wait for his answer.

"You think McGill's lying to us, Mickey?" I said. "Maybe he didn't even go out to the creek to look for the body. Maybe he said he did but he didn't. Why would he lie to us?"

"People lie to cover up something they don't want you to find out," Abby said. "What's McGill hiding?"

"McGill's not a liar," Mickey said. "Not a big liar anyway. He's one of the better ones over there, and he's been around for years. He's got a good reputation. Some of those cops can be as dumb as a football bat. Not McGill."

"So what explains this?" Abby said. "We see the body, we tell McGill. He goes out to the creek and doesn't find the body. We go back and – *magic* –there's the body. Very same place, too."

"Let's assume McGill is telling the truth," I said. "That means someone moved the body after we saw it. And put it back in the shack after McGill left. Is that what happened?"

"If it is, some of those creek-running rednecks like playing around with a corpse," Mickey said. "Somebody is keeping a close watch on that shack."

"People will do anything to hide the truth if it keeps them from going to prison," Abby said. "We've got to get to the truth. When we do there'll be no more missing girls."

"Is there anything you two saw that would lead to an ID of the body?" Mickey said. "Anything you saw this morning that you didn't see before?"

"Shit, Mickey, we saw less of a person this morning than we did the first time," I said. "We told you about the buzzards, remember? We told you what they did to the man's face."

"Could you see any articles of clothing?" Mickey said. "Anything specific?"

"I think he was wearing a white T-shirt," Abby said. "Some kind of white shirt. Maybe jeans, too. I can't say for certain, Mickey. Half of his chest had been eaten away. We weren't paying attention to what he might've been wearing."

Mickey hit his cigarette hard again, twice this time. Blew more smoke over our heads.

"Okay, goddamnit, here's what I want you two to do," Mickey said. "Talk to McGill again. Tell him what you saw this morning. Get him on record involving the body. We may write a story about it. I don't know yet. Let me think it through. But you contact McGill. Got it?"

"We got it," I said.

"You got good notes, don't you?" Mickey said.

"We do Mickey," Abby said. "I've taken notes from both times we've seen the body. I've got it all."

"I don't have any notes, Mickey," I said. "Too busy throwing up."

CHAPTER 32

Now we had two reasons to interview again Detective McGill at the APD. We needed to learn if he had ordered any interviews in connection with the Maria Rios murder investigation, as he said he was going to do, and could he give us any information based on those interviews.

And we needed to tell him we returned to the creek and saw the dead body again. In the same place in the shack. We'd give him an opportunity to comment on what we saw because, as Mickey said, we were considering running a story. You could call it the mystery of the disappearing body.

If the buzzards continued with their meal at the shack, there wouldn't be much of a body to recover. We needed to get to McGill as soon as possible. We needed to act fast.

We were at Abby's desk trying to determine our next move on the story. She bought two bottled Cokes from the red machine in the newsroom and gave me one. They were cold. There were small particles of ice dripping on them.

"Here, John, I think your stomach needs this now. It'll do you some good. It's good and cold."

"Thanks, I needed this. I needed it more than I thought I did."

"Johnny Boy, I'm always taking care of you."

I took another drink and sat the Coke on Abby's desk next to a book of poetry that included works from Edgar Allen Poe. Abby loved her poetry and was never far from it. She always had a book of poetry on her desk and another in her purse.

"I'm sure he would be inspired by what we saw this morning," I said. "Blood. Guts. Death."

"Who's he?"

"Poe. The poet Poe."

"Forget about him, John. We need to get to McGill. What do you want to do? You want to walk over there and see if we can catch him at his office? Or you want to call him?"

"You're close to the phone," I said. "Have at it."

I needed to enjoy the Coke and let my stomach settle. My ability to concentrate was limited.

Abby didn't hesitate. She kept next to her phone a white index card taped to her desk with several important numbers. She dialed McGill's number as I continued drinking. She opened her notepad to a clean page and held a black pen in her right hand. She was ready.

McGill answered the phone a few seconds later. She took notes and I listened. She was thorough in her questions and her follow-ups. A few of his answers she repeated to ensure accuracy. She spent about ten minutes on the phone with him based on the big black and white clock in the newsroom. She turned to me when she hung up.

"Well, let's hear it," I said. "Tell me everything he said."

Abby said McGill had no new leads on the Maria Rios murder investigation. His investigators had spoken with Pearl, Big Foot, and the landowner in Mitchell County, the one who owns the land on the creek where we saw the longhouse and the dead body.

McGill was convinced they knew nothing of a body or someone being murdered on the creek. He had no reason to believe any of them were connected with the Maria Rios case or any other crime.

McGill told Abby he had contacted the sheriff's office in Brooks County to discuss the two missing girls and whether they were connected with Maria Rios. He didn't know the answer to that question yet. The investigations were continuing.

"Back up a second," I said. "He said he talked to Big Foot? Is that what he said?"

"Correct."

"Remember what Sugar Baby told us last night? Said Big Foot had not gotten back from his fishing trip to Panama City. Told us that last night. Said he was overdue. Remember?"

"That's right, I remember."

"So, when and where did McGill's investigators speak with Big Foot?" I said. "Did you ask him specifically?"

"John, I did not. Maybe I should've but I didn't."

"And nobody knows anything about the body? None of the people they interviewed?"

"That's what he said," Abby said.

"Of course that's what he said. There is no dead body. It's all in our heads, right Abby? We didn't see a body, did we?"

"I'm starting to feel the same way, John. This is weird. Very weird. McGill's answers. They weren't very convincing."

"It would be hard to interview Big Foot if he was still in Panama City," I said. "Don't you agree?"

"Not unless they went down to the Gulf," Abby said. "Harder still if he *was* the body at that shack. Don't you agree?"

"Yeah, I'd like to see that interview. But we're stretching things here, don't you think? A big, big stretch."

"Somebody was killed and buried out there. Maybe somebody we know. Somebody we've seen recently."

"What did he say when you told him we saw the body again this morning on the creek?" I said. "What was his reaction to that?"

"He said he'd send out a couple of his people this afternoon to take another look in the shack."

"You believe him?"

"Do I believe him?" Abby said. "What do you think? You think I believe him?"

"I think we don't know what the hell is going on with McGill. It's possible the body was moved when he went out there the first time. It's also possible he said he went out there, but didn't. Why would he lie to us, Abby?"

"Like I said, people lie to cover things up. I want to believe he went out the first time. I want to believe he'll go back today. Very hard to accept that the body was moved, then put back in the shack and now will be moved again so McGill can't see it?"

"Sounds like a crazy-ass movie to me," I said.

"My thoughts exactly."

"If they go out there today and find the body, it won't be much of one," I said. "They better hurry."

"Right. Those buzzards, the way they were going, are not going to leave much. Maybe they won't eat his pants and shoes. If he was wearing shoes."

"Pants and shoes. That's probably all they'll leave."

"John, that's why *we've* got to go back there today. We may have to get that body ourselves so it can be identified. If the cops aren't going to do it, we have to."

"What! What in the hell did you just say?"

"You heard me. My words were clear."

"I used to think you were willing to do everything you could to find out who's doing all this so no other girls would get hurt. Now I'm beginning to think you may be going crazy. Too much sun, Abby. You need to stay out of the sun for a while."

"If it's crazy to want to help someone, then, yes, I've lost my mind. Blame the sun if you want to, I don't care. Besides, can we depend on McGill? You know the answer to that question."

"Are you *really* saying we should go back to the creek, get the body, and bring it to the police department?" I said. "You want to be an undertaker now? That's your new career?"

"No, I'm a newspaper reporter. Okay, maybe we don't get the body. Maybe we go out there and take some pictures of it. Maybe that's what we do."

"So now you think McGill is involved in this?" I said. "You think he's lying to us all along?"

"I don't know where the truth is right now, you don't either. But I do believe the body is the key to all of this. If McGill's not going to do his job, for whatever reason, we need to act."

"How about going back out there and just taking some pictures of whatever's left of that man? There's your evidence we can take to the police. I threw up once, like Mickey said, maybe that'll be the only time."

"Good. I'm glad you agree."

"If we take the body, Abby, then we can be charged with breaking the law. You're not supposed move evidence from a crime scene."

"I've heard that somewhere. We can't worry about that right now, John."

"What do you want me to worry about?"

"Right now, I don't want you to worry. I want you to call Charlie Moon and explain our situation to him. Maybe he's got a contact in the FBI that can help us. I called McGill, now you call Charlie."

"He's hard a man to track down sometimes. He stays on the move in his territory."

"Call him, John. Call him now."

CHAPTER 33

I got behind Abby's desk and called Charlie Moon at his home in Thomasville. Abby stood close to me, leaning toward the phone in an effort to hear what Charlie was saying. I could feel and smell her sweet breath.

We were fortunate to reach him. Sometimes it irritated the shit out of Mickey because Charlie's whereabouts were unpredictable. But he always produced good stories and that's what mattered the most to Mickey. "Charlie, this is John Maynard. Can you talk? I need to talk to you."

"Yeah, just doin' a little political story on the Seminole County Commission. It can wait. If you need to talk, I need to listen. Whatta you got?"

I told Charlie what we had seen that morning on the creek, and then I explained the interview Abby had with McGill. The situation was urgent we believed. We were losing confidence in McGill and the APD. The body might lead us to whoever killed Maria Rios and abducted the two girls in Brooks County. We couldn't wait. We had to act now.

"I understand it all and I agree," Charlie said. "What can I do to help you two up there?"

"You told us you had an FBI source," I said. "We need help Charlie. Do you think your source would help us? We need to show your source, or someone in the FBI, the body. We need to move fast, if we don't there won't be much of a body to show after the buzzards are through."

"I reckon that dead man smells worse than the ass-end of a shit-covered goat," Charlie said.

"Worse than that, Charlie. I promise you."

"I've seen and smelled a few bodies in this business," Charlie said. "It's like the man said, 'Buzzards got to eat, same as worms.' "

Charlie was quoting a line from the movie, *The Outlaw Josey Wales.* Clint Eastwood, who played Wales, said the line after killing a couple of men. Wales didn't bury the men but left their bodies exposed to the natural world. Buzzards got to eat, same as worms. I'd seen the move twice and loved it.

But the dead body we'd seen on the creek was real, not make believe as in the movie. Time was slipping away.

"That's a great movie, Charlie," I said. "I love Eastwood but we've got to act now."

"Glad you recognize the movie. That Eastwood was a bad-ass sumbitch…"

"Can you help us?" I said.

"You in the office?"

"Yeah, I'm at Abby's desk."

"Stay put. Stay by the phone. Let me make a couple of calls, and I'll get right back to you. Buzzards got to eat, same as worms. I won't be long."

"We'll be waiting."

Abby stepped away from my side and spoke after I hung up.

"What did he say? I couldn't hear him? Is he going to make some calls for us?"

"He said, 'Buzzards got to eat, same as worms.' "

"What? What does that mean?"

"That's a line from *The Outlaw Josey Wells*," I said. "We watched it together."

"I don't want to hear about the movie. Is he going to help us?"

"Yes, he'll call back in a few minutes."

I finished my Coke and read the morning paper, and Abby did the same. It was difficult to concentrate on my reading. I couldn't get the image out of my mind of the buzzard that had the human colon dangling from its mouth. Most people don't have that experience when they're working. We were just lucky.

Abby's phone rang ten minutes after I finished talking with Charlie the first time. I answered before the first ring ended.

"Charlie? What'd you find out?"

"Here's the deal. Listen up."

I had a pen and notepad at the ready as Charlie spoke. FBI agent Edward "Ed" Hanahan had been living in Albany since the 1960s when he was transferred there from Boston. The Bureau relocated him during the upheaval of the Albany Movement, the local arm of the national Civil Rights Movement. Hanahan was one of several agents then who investigated violence from whites in South Georgia aimed at blacks during that period.

Afterwards he stayed in Albany and continued working with the FBI, and Charlie had met him in the mid-1970s. He had been a good source for Charlie over the years and the two had developed a friendship. Hanahan was in his forties, married, and had seven children. He was devoted to his family, the Bureau, and the Catholic Church. Charlie said he was a "straight-shooter" who was loyal to the truth.

"He's a no-bullshit guy," Charlie said. "I told him the situation. He's aware of the Maria Rios case and has done some legwork on the missing girls in Brooks County. Been involved with some interviews down there."

"Can he help us today?"

"Said he would."

Charlie gave me Hanahan's phone number and after I hung up with Charlie, I called the FBI agent at home. He was off that day having worked five straight twelve-hour shifts. I had a quick conversation with Hanahan, who said he could meet us at Warren Crew's house on the creek in about fifteen minutes.

I gave him directions and Warren's address. He said he'd bring a body bag and masks. Standard tools of his job. That conversation was over in less than a minute.

"Abby, the agent's name is Ed Hanahan. He's going to meet us at Warren's in fifteen minutes. Charlies said we can fully trust him. He's bringing a body bag just in case the buzzards left enough for identification. And he has been working on the case of the two missing girls from Brooks County. The child sex-ring case."

"Good, John. Maybe this is the break we need. We've got to get out of here and get to the creek."

"What are we going to tell Mickey?"

"You leave that to me. I'll handle this. Just grab my camera and be ready to get out of here."

Abby walked to Mickey's desk, spoke to him, and he nodded his head. She waved at me to walk out of the newsroom with her.

"Well? What did you tell him?"

"I told him I was worried about you because you threw up this morning. You're weak and needed something in your stomach. I was going to take you to get some food."

"You lied to Mickey?" I said. "You know how much he despises a liar."

"No, I didn't lie to Mickey. I am going to take you to get a hamburger. You do need some food. Then we're going to meet the FBI agent at the creek. I told Mickey the truth."

"I love an honest woman."

"Let's go."

CHAPTER 34

Abby had me stop at McDonald restaurant on Slappey Boulevard where she bought me a cheeseburger, fries, and a Coke. She said she wasn't hungry and got nothing for herself. She drove my car while I ate.

I needed the food. But if I saw the buzzards again eating human flesh, the hamburger and fries might end up like my Cheerios. I ate it all anyway and in a hurry. In a hurry was the way Abby was driving to the creek.

"You're going to get pulled over by the cops if you don't slow down," I said. "Then what will we do? What's your plan then?"

"Good, maybe the cops will come with us and help."

"If I told you lately that you can be a smart..."

"Smart what? Smart reporter?"

"Yes, that's right. That's what I was going to say. And I love you. I was going to say that, too."

"I thought that's what you were going to say," she said.

Waiting for us at Warren's house was FBI agent Ed Hanahan. I did not see Warren's jeep or the yellow Volkswagen beetle that his girlfriend was driving the other night. But I did see the dark blue Ford LTD that Hanahan had arrived in.

He stood next to his vehicle holding a thick, black body bag and three white masks. The masks were the kind a surgeon might use during an operation or a millworker protecting himself from lint. We would use them to keep the smell of death off of us.

Hanahan saw us pull in Warren's driveway, and we came to a stop next to his vehicle.

He looked to be in his late-forties and close to six feet tall. He had the look of an athlete with broad shoulders and thick arms. Maybe he played football growing up in Massachusetts, maybe hockey. He had a revolver strapped around his left shoulder in a brown leather holster and I couldn't tell for sure, but it looked like a snub-nose thirty-eight. He wore it high, not on his waistline like in a cowboy movie.

The introductions were quick and Hanahan's handshake felt like punishment. He smiled when he did it.

The sun was high and hot and Hanahan was wearing a ball cap, gray boots, a white UMASS T-shirt and khakis. We were dressed casual and comfortable, too. Both of us had caps on for protection from the sun. We walked straight and fast to Warren's dock and into the boat.

I pulled the rope once, and the motor started. Going up the creek full throttle, I thought of how crowded it's going to be coming back with a full body bag. Three live adults and one dead one in the small johnboat. But the trip was short.

"Mr. Hanahan, how long you been with the FBI?" Abby said.

"A little more than twenty years, but please call me Ed," he said. "Was sent down during the 1960s and the civil rights unrest. I wanted to stay and the Bureau let me. I like it here. A much better place today than it was back then. I've got lots of family in Massachusetts, but I don't miss the snow and ice. You haven't been with the paper long, have you?"

"Just a few of years," Abby said. "We started about the same time."

"I read your work," Hanahan said. "When Charlie Moon mentioned your names, I recognized them. Both of them. You two seem to know what you're doing. You're good at it."

"Sometimes we know what we're doing," I said. "Not on this story. We've gotten ourselves into a mess. Damn fine mess."

"You two are in the same kind of business I'm in."

"What do you mean Mr...I mean Ed?" Abby said.

"We're all trying to clean up the mess. We believe in what we're doing. I like doing what I'm doing, and I'd guess the same about you two. We both see a lot of messes."

"You're right, Ed," I said. "And we got one helluva a mess on the Kinchafoonee. One helluva mess."

"I know. We've been on these boys for a while now," Hanahan said. "Just haven't put together all the dots. Looks like you two may be out in front of us on this."

"I hope when we leave here today, the dots are all in line," Abby said. "We can't lose anymore girls. It's got to stop today. It's got to stop."

"Maybe this is the lead that will do it, Abby," Hanahan said. "Let's go see what's out here."

On the same side of the creek as the deer trail that led to the shack, I saw a big gator sunbathing, maybe a seven footer. It was all green, gray, and metallic. I didn't say anything about it and nobody else did, either.

I looked overhead expecting to see the buzzards we had seen earlier in the day, but didn't see any. Maybe both breakfast and lunch had ended. The water was low and smooth. The way it had been since the morning I saw Big Foot talking to Whitfield along the creek. The same morning Pearl threatened to whip my ass. That's when all this began.

The deer trail came into view a minute after we saw the big gator. We had seen no other boats on the water. We had seen nobody else. I eased the boat to the bank, and we got out in a hurry and pulled the boat behind the tall weeds and blackberry bushes. It was a familiar activity.

Abby took the lead on the trail, I was behind her and Hanahan last. He had the body bag and masks.

I heard quick movement in a tall willow tree and was startled by it. I stopped and looked up. Two buzzards were sitting atop the tree, looking at us. Hanahan saw what I saw.

"You recognize those two from this morning?" he said. "Their bellies look full, don't they?"

"Yeah, they were probably involved in the breakfast buffet," I said. "Too fat to fly off now."

"What are you two looking at?" Abby said.

She had stopped walking and turned to face us.

"Just a couple of our friends from this morning," I said. "Fat and happy."

"I hope that's the only two we see," Abby said. "Let's keep going."

We came to the clearing where the shack was and stopped when it came in full view. The awful smell became apparent. The death smell. Hanahan gave us each a mask and we all put them on. Then he picked up a long oak stick and we moved on.

We walked to the cabin and through the front door that was still wide open, the way it was when we had left earlier that day. There were three buzzards standing over the body but none of them were eating of human flesh. They turned to look at us.

What the hell you doin' back here? Leave us alone.

Hanahan beat the oak stick on the floor as he herded the buzzards out of the cabin. He circled them as a rancher on horseback would cattle.

"Go! Get out of here! Get!" he said.

Two of the buzzards moved from the body and out the door. The third stood its ground, maybe not finished with breakfast or lunch. Hanahan tapped that one on the head with his stick. Then the bird fluttered out into the grass with its companions. He gave the FBI agent an ugly look as he left the shack.

Now it was just us and the body. The mask was keeping the worse of the smell off of me. The sight of the eaten-over body was still sickening, but it looked about the same as it did earlier. I still couldn't recognize the victim.

Hanahan placed the FBI body bag on the floor and unzipped it. From his pocket he pulled white latex gloves for all of us and we put them on. By himself he pulled the dead man up from the dirt until the body was lying on the wooden cabin floor next to the bag. It was not difficult for him to do this alone. He was a strong man. Now came our part.

"Help me lift him in, and we'll get out of here," Hanahan said.

"Let's get it done, John," Abby said.

The three of us lifted the body from the black garbage bag and placed it in the FBI bag. Then Hanahan zipped the bag tight. We took off our gloves and returned them to Hanahan. He put them back in his pocket.

"John, I'm going to need you to help me carry him back to the boat," Hanahan said.

"What about me?" Abby said. "I can help, too. What do you want me to do?"

"I know you can," Hanahan said. "If either one of us needs a break, you're it."

"Okay, just let me know," Abby said.

"Let's go," I said. "I'm ready to get the hell out of here and not come back. Ever."

Abby took the lead on the walk back to the creek as I helped Hanahan carry the dead man in the black bag. The bag was as black as the buzzards that had feasted on the body. There were four buzzards now in the grass outside of the shack and they watched as we carried away their meal.

They made no attempt to disrupt what we had to do. Whatever the man had weighed before he was killed had been reduced by what the buzzards had eaten. He was not a heavy load.

We were a hundred yards or so from the boat before anyone spoke.

"John?" Abby said.

"Yeah, what is it?"

"Did you see his feet? Did you see how big his feet are?"

"I did and I knew you did too," I said. "Chuck Taylor Converse. Black. I've seen Big Foot wear those at the Monkey Palace more than once. Looked like size fifteen."

"That's what I thought," Abby said. "Hard to miss those feet."

I could see the johnboat and the creek ahead. Carrying the dead man had been easier than I thought. We didn't need Abby to trade off with us. She was ready had we needed her. Like I said, Hanahan was a damn strong man. The kind of guy you want to share a heavy load with. And he appeared to be the kind of guy who wouldn't take any shit from anyone. Just like Charlie Moon said.

He had heard Abby and me talking about Big Foot.

"I saw those shoes, too," Hanahan said. "Hard to miss. Big Foot has been on our radar. I've seen pictures of him."

"Do you think it's him you're carrying?" Abby said. "What do you think?"

"Hard to say," Hanahan said. "There's not enough left of his face for me to make a decent judgement. His shoes? There's other people who have big feet and wear Converse. We'll have to let the boys in the white jackets figure it out. The boys in the lab."

We made it to the johnboat and laid the body on the ground next to it. We pulled the boat into the Kinchafoonee and Abby steadied it as Hanahan and me loaded the body. We laid the body across the boat in the middle with his head hanging over one side of the boat and his big feet hanging over the opposite side. Hanahan got in the boat next to the body to keep it stationary on the way to Warren's. Abby got in next, then I did.

I started the motor again, and we were off.

"We need to get to a phone," Hanahan said. "I need to get an ambulance out here to pick him up and get him to the coroner's office. I need to call my office, too. Do you think your friend is home now? Can we get into his house?"

"Even if he's not, we can still get in," I said. "There's a lot of things Warren doesn't believe in and one of them is using locks."

"If folks are being shot and buried near his backyard, he might want to reconsider his position on door locks," Hanahan said.

"I'll be sure to tell him," I said.

The first shot hit me in my right arm above the elbow. I saw the blood stream down my arm before I felt the pain of the bullet. I had never been shot. Never been shot at.

The second shot ricocheted off the motor and maybe into the water. The third shot hit Hanahan in the chest.

"In the water!" Hanahan said. "Get in the water!"

The three of us leapt out of the boat and into the creek. Then the body slid off the boat and disappeared into the water. From underwater I could hear more gunshots and still feel the blood and the sting from the bullet in my arm.

CHAPTER 35

I couldn't tell for sure where the gunshots were coming from but knew for certain my right arm was almost useless. It hurt like hell now. I swam to top water hard using my left arm and legs. I knew the creek wasn't deep. And I knew it didn't take much water to drown in.

I saw that Abby and Hanahan were near me after my head was above water.

Then two more gunshots were fired at us and they seem to come from the other side of the creek near the deer trail. They were both misses.

Hanahan pointed to the bank of the creek opposite from where the shots were coming from and where a large water oak had fallen into the water. It was about thirty-five feet away. We swam most of the way underwater.

Abby reached the tree first and grabbed onto it. She was full strength and had not been shot. I could see that Hanahan's UMASS white T-shirt was soaked in blood that matched the red lettering on it. He had been shot in his upper right chest about an inch or so from his shoulder.

"Let's go!" Abby said. "We've got to get into the woods. Let's go! We've got to get away from the creek."

The tree line was only about ten feet from the water. Once we got into the trees and ran for several seconds, I stopped. Now the three of us were behind a cluster of water oaks thick with gray Spanish moss.

"We've got to keep going, John," she said. "Farther into the woods."

"Wait, Abby, wait. Just wait."

Then she looked at us and saw we had been shot.

"Oh, God, John, I didn't know. *How bad? How bad?*"

"I'm okay. I think the bullet went straight through. I can run, but my right arm can't do much. Ed looks worse."

"Ed, can you make it into the woods?" Abby said. "We've got to keep moving."

"You're right," Ed said. "We need to put some distance between us and whoever's doing the shooting. I can go. Let's all stay as low as you can. Let's move!"

I heard no other shots as we ran through the honeysuckle and blackberry bushes and the pines and oaks. We ran farther into the woods and away from whoever was trying to kill us. We ran for about three or four minutes before stopping behind a dozen large water oaks that towered over other trees in the woods. We were exhausted and sat in the tall grass at the base of the trees.

I didn't think once about water moccasins. I could hardly breathe. It took us several seconds before we were able to talk. We were looking in the direction of the creek from behind the trees.

"Let me see, John," Abby said. "Let me see your arm."

The bleeding had stopped. It looked as if the bullet had gone through my arm. It wasn't fatal. But I couldn't lift my arm above my head without terrible pain. I probably couldn't use an ink pen with my right hand.

Abby knew I had a red bandana in my pants pocket and she removed it and tied it around my arm where the bullet had entered. It felt a little better because of what she did. I sat back against the base of a tree.

"How bad is it, Ed?" Abby said. "What do you need me to do?"

"I'm not going to die on you, but I'm not much good right now," Hanahan said. "I need something to press on this wound. I'm still leaking a little bit. I need a piece of cloth or something."

"John, are you carrying that old pocketknife?" Abby said. "The one that used to belong to your grandfather?"

"Yeah, same pocket."

Abby got my pocketknife and cut off the blue Atlanta Braves T-shirt I was wearing. She folded it three times and placed it on Hanahan's right shoulder where the bullet had entered. She did it as if she was an experienced war-time nurse.

"Thanks, Abby," he said. "I'll keep the pressure on it, but we've got to find a way out of these woods and away from who's shooting at us. I'm like John, my right arm is useless. I can't even raise my gun let alone shoot…"

"*I know you're back there!*" the man said. "*I should've kilt you and your bitch when I had the chance. You rotten piece of goddamn shit!*"

"It's Pearl," I said. "I know that voice. It's Pearl. He's been wanting to kill me for a while. Now he wants to kill Abby, too."

"And me," Hanahan said.

I saw Pearl moving closer to us and using the big pines for cover. He had his pearl-handled gun in his right hand. I couldn't smell his nasty liquor-breath but that's probably what he had. He was pressing in on us. He was pissed.

"Before I shoot ya in the head, I'm goin' cut ya tongues out," Pearl said. "That's what ya get for talkin' bad about me. Ya cocksucker."

"Abby, hand me my gun," Hanahan said.

His sub-nose was under his left shoulder and because of the pain he was unable to use his right arm. Abby gave Hanahan his gun and with his left hand he fired two un-aimed shots in Pearl's direction. Hanahan was right handed. We were in big trouble.

I saw Pearl's movement behind a big pine about fifty yards from us. For several seconds there was silence after Hanahan's shots.

"Pearl, this is Ed Hanahan with the FBI," Hanahan said. "If you put the gun away and talk to me, we can work this thing out. We don't want anyone to get hurt out here. There's been enough of that."

"Hurt?" Pearl said. "I'm goin' kill ya, dickhead. I don't give a god-damn if your FBI, GBI, IGB or BBI. I don't give a rat's ass who the fuck ya are."

Pearl fired two shots in our direction and they both hit a tree ten or fifteen feet above our heads. We were within his range but protected by the water oaks for now.

"Give me the gun, Ed," Abby said. "Let me have it."

"What?" Hanahan said.

"Let me have your gun," Abby said. "You can't use it. Neither can John. He doesn't know much about guns. I know that for a fact."

"And you do?" Hanahan said.

"Yes, thanks to my father. I can point it and shoot it straight. You two can't. Besides, you got a better plan?"

"I wish I had," Hanahan said.

Hanahan gave his gun to Abby. She looked at the chamber and counted bullets. Hanahan had extra bullets on his holster and Abby replaced the ones he had used.

"Now what?" Hanahan said.

"You two keep talking to him," Abby said. "Keep his mind occupied the best you can. I'm going to get to him hopefully in a way that he won't see me."

"What the hell are you going to do?" I said. "I don't like this, Abby. *Jesus Christ I don't like this!*"

"I don't like where we are either, John. I'm going to try to get us out of here alive. Just keep talking to Pearl."

"Abby, I just don't..."

"Just keep talking to Pearl," she said. "Just do what I ask."

"You sure you know how to use that gun?" Hanahan said.

Abby didn't answer. She was gone. Abby was running gun-in-hand behind the water oaks where we were and in the opposite direction from Pearl. I watched her for several yards and then she was out of sight. The area was dense with pine, oak, hickory, and cherry and tall underbrush. She was making her own trail.

She was going to circle back toward Pearl and the creek, I thought. That was her plan. To try to surprise him.

"Pearl, this is John Maynard. I'm sorry about all of this. Can't we find a way to work it out? What can I do to work it out with you, Pearl?"

"Work it out?" Pearl said. "That's right shithead, we'll work it out as soon as I put a bullet in ya head. That's how we're goin' work it out."

"Pearl, you don't want to kill us," Hanahan said. "The Bureau gets pissed off if you kill one of their agents. You don't want the FBI on your ass, do you? You've already killed one man and buried him out here."

"That stupid shithead had it comin'," Pearl said. "He wouldn't listen to me. Ya got it comin', too, goddamnit."

"Pearl, if you come after us, I promise you, you won't kill us," Hanahan said. "It'll be the other way around."

"Ya a stupid dickhead, too," Pearl said. "These are my woods. I decide who lives or dies out here. Not ya, fuckhead."

"I'll tell you what, Pearl," Hanahan said. "If you put your gun away and cooperate, I promise you I'll work with the judge to get your sentence reduced. I promise. You have my word."

"Ain't goin' be no goddamn sentence!"

Pearl shot twice at us again but missed. Now Hanahan and I were lying flat on the ground and looking around the base of separate trees toward Pearl. I saw him move closer to us. Soon I would smell his breath.

I looked for Abby but didn't see any sign of her. I was hoping Pearl couldn't see her, either.

CHAPTER 36

The three gunshots came in quick succession. They made me jump from where I was lying as if I were a child and my uncle had scared me in the dark. I had a couple of uncles who were good at doing such things.

Pop! Pop! Pop!

Nothing but silence for almost thirty seconds before the moaning began. It was Abby, I thought. Pearl had shot her. It sounded like Abby.

"*That redneck sonofabitch!*" I said.

Hanahan turned to look at me. He was still lying on the ground behind the giant oak tree. And he was still pressing my T-shirt against his bullet wound. The bleeding had not entirely stopped.

"*Abby! Abby!*" I said.

No reply.

"I've got to go to her, Ed. She's been shot. Pearl shot her. She's been shot."

"No, wait," Hanahan said. "You can't go out there. He'll shoot you, too. Hold on, damn it! We need a plan."

"I can't wait for a plan. Abby needs me."

I got up from the ground and ran to where the shots had come from. I was an easy in-coming target for Pearl. I saw a large curl of gun smoke rising in the trees where I was headed. Seeing it made me run faster.

Then I saw a body lying on the ground and another person standing near it. Pearl had killed her. Goddamn him.

But then the smoke cleared.

"Oh, John, you're okay now. We're all okay. We're going to make it now. It's all over now."

I rushed to Abby and hugged her hard, but I could only use my left arm. She hugged me with her left arm too as she kept Hanahan's snub-nose thirty-eight in her right hand. God Almighty she felt good.

We held tight for several seconds and when we released each other, I turned to Pearl who was lying on the ground. Abby had moved his gun far out of reach.

"Whatta ya lookin' at?" Pearl said. "I'm still goin' kill ya and that bitch that shot me. Ya wait and see. I'll make ya dead one day. Gonna cut ya tongue out just like I said. Ya little fuckhead."

I said nothing to Pearl and looked back at Abby. I could tell he had been shot in the upper right thigh and right shoulder. He was lying flat on the ground with his head tilted up so he could see me when he threatened our lives again. He was next to a small magnolia tree that had a dozen or so white blooms. It was odd how beautiful they looked despite the violence that surrounded them.

"Ya hear me boy!" Pearl said. *"Goddamn ya, ya better hear me."*

"No, Pearl, you aren't going to kill us," I said. "You'll be dead before you get out of prison. I bet you a bottle of Jack on that."

"Ya better get me some help, or I'm gonna bleed to death in these goddamn woods."

I ignored Pearl again and looked at Abby.

"How?"

"I came up behind him around that big tree over there," Abby said. "He didn't see. He didn't hear me."

She pointed to a big live oak about thirty feet from where Pearl was lying. Three adults could've hidden behind it and not been seen. "And then?" I said.

"I spoke first, almost in a whisper, but he heard me," Abby said. "I said if he put down his gun, the FBI would go easy on him. He turned and came toward the tree and fired. I fired twice. That was it."

"Holy shit, Abby! Holy damn shit."

"Yeah, you could say that and I would agree."

Then we heard Hanahan walking toward us. He was still using my blue T-shirt to put pressure on his wound. The shirt was more red than blue. He stopped next to Abby and looked at her.

"Your father must've taught you well," Hanahan said. "We could use you in the Bureau."

"I was always a good student, Ed," she said. "I'll stick with being a reporter. That's what I love."

"I understand," Hanahan said. "If you change your mind, we need to talk."

"What do we do now?" I said.

"You two stay here with Pearl," Abby said. "He won't give you any problems. I'll make it to Warren's house and get us some help. It shouldn't take me long."

"Come here before you go," I said. "Come here to me."

She pressed against me and we hugged tight again. Tighter than before. She had given Hanahan his gun and used both arms for the hug. She kissed my neck a few times and I kissed hers.

"If something ever happened to you Abby…"

"Don't even say it, John. Nothing's going to happen to me. Nothing's going to happen to us. I'm here with you where I belong."

"God, I love you," I said.

"You are my very, Johnny Boy. Always will be."

"And I thought I knew everything about you," I said.

"What do you mean?"

"Running through the woods and shooting a madman who was trying to kill us," I said. "That's what I mean."

"John, don't you know a woman has got to do what she has to."

"I do now. She did and I'm damn proud and impressed."

"Good," Abby said. "Let's keep it that way."

"You never told me you could shoot a gun," I said. "You never told me your dad taught you how."

"Every woman's got some secrets and some things are better when you find them out on our own," Abby said. "Through experience. Don't you agree?"

"I do now."

With that Abby left me and Hanahan with Pearl and began her walk through the woods to Warren's house. It couldn't be more than a quarter of a mile, I thought. I wasn't worried about her after what I had seen her do in the woods.

"Here, take this just in case," Hanahan said. "We've got Pearl's gun and he's not going to be a problem."

Hanahan gave his gun to Abby for the second time that day.

"All right, just in case," she said.

After a few steps away from me, she stopped, turned around, looked at me and formed these words without speaking them: *I love you.*

I said the same but out loud to her, then she disappeared into the woods again.

CHAPTER 37

The story of the torture and murder of Maria Rios played out the way I'm going to tell it now.

On her way to Warren's house to call the police and an ambulance, Abby met Detective McGill and a couple of his officers in a gray APD aluminum boat heading toward the deer trail. They were doing what McGill said he'd do. Return to the shack in search of the body.

They would not have found it that time had they gotten there. Now the body was at the bottom of the Kinchafoonee Creek.

McGill talked with Abby and then returned to his squad car and radioed for help. Abby stayed at Warren's while McGill and his two men came to where Hanahan and I were watching Pearl.

McGill got us back to Warren's house by boat and a few minutes later two ambulances arrived. Then a team of divers came to the creek that afternoon and retrieved the body.

Hanahan and I were transported to Phoebe Putney Hospital in Albany in one of the ambulances. McGill and a couple of his officers rode in the other ambulance with Pearl. McGill contacted the FBI and a couple of agents were headed to the hospital.

Doctors treated me in the emergency room along with Hanahan, and they released us later that afternoon. Pearl was admitted because of the seriousness of his wounds.

"I wanna call my goddamn lawyer!"

Pearl spoke those words, according to McGill, after the bullets were removed and he awoke in his hospital room later that day.

Hiram "Pearl" Woodfin took the advice of his lawyer, who told him if his case went to trial authorities would seek the death penalty.

Pearl admitted to murder, child sex-trafficking, drug trafficking, and several other offenses. He confessed to it all, and he would be sentenced in the weeks ahead.

Pearl would likely die in prison. The same thing I told him after Abby shot him.

Pearl didn't kill Maria Rios. And the body that had been buried under the shack near the witch tree was not Big Foot. It was Shiloh Felton. Or "Hi-Low" as Pearl and Big Foot called him when he was stoned on bourbon and cocaine. Shiloh had helped kidnap and transport teenage girls. The sex-ring involved a handful of other rotten men. Authorities would later arrest them at an old farmhouse in Mitchell County and some outside of Georgia.

Pearl and Big Foot made Shiloh feel a part of the team. Paid him good money, too. Shiloh had felt important for the first time in his life.

Big Foot was arrested that evening during happy hour at the Monkey Palace after returning earlier in the day from Panama City. Some happy hour for Big Foot. He brought no fish back but had a duffel bag full of cocaine from his contacts on the Gulf. All six monkeys watched as police escorted Big Foot out of his nightclub in handcuffs. The music and dancing stopped when the cops came in. Big Foot turned the operation of the club over to Sugar Baby, who refused to hear a word against him. To Sugar Baby, Big Foot was "nuthin' but a good man."

Police charged Big Foot with a number of crimes but not the murder of Shiloh. Pearl killed Shiloh on his own and this is how it went down.

Pearl said he had shot Shiloh in the head and buried him under the shack next to the witch tree. He did it after Shiloh dumped Maria's body in the woods off Palmyra Road. Pearl did remove Shiloh's body and replace it. That was why it wasn't there when McGill searched the shack.

"That dumb fuck was going to tell the cops what the senator did to the girl," Pearl told the police. "The boy Shiloh was just as dumb as a dead possum. I figured if I didn't kill 'im, he'd tell ya every goddamn thing. He went crazy when I told him to dump the body, and he found out what the senator did to her. Big Foot had nothin' to do with killin' Shiloh. It was all me."

Pearl's details filled out the story. He told police they scouted for young girls who were working the fields in South Georgia. They figured the police wouldn't be so eager to investigate the disappearance of brown girls from a different country. He also said that some of their clients, like Senator Jefferson Beauregard Whitfield, particularly prized teenage girls from Central America.

Pearl and Big Foot both saw Maria Rios on a scouting expedition and were struck by her beauty. They kidnapped her and took her to the longhouse. There Senator Whitfield, the family values politician, raped and killed her in room number seven.

According to Pearl's story, Whitfield had almost beaten to death a fifteen-year old prostitute in Honduras. On a couple of occasions at the longhouse, the senator had to be restrained by Pearl from seriously hurting girls he had paid for.

"I called J.B. 'The Wild Man from the Sudan' because he liked to git rough with 'em," Pearl said. "He done got too rough. He never would listen to me. I told 'im one day he'd go too far. And goddamnit he did."

FBI agents and Mitchell County lawmen arrested Whitfield at his home in Camilla the same day Abby shot Pearl. They arrived at about eight-thirty as the senator was watching a television program with his wife and children.

When Whitfield saw the flashing lights in his driveway, he stood up from where he was sitting on the sofa next to his wife and spoke to his family.

"I'll be going away for a long, long time now. I did some bad things. Some awful things."

He opened the front door and stood on the porch as FBI agents handcuffed him, put him in their car and drove away. The day after Whitfield was arrested, his wife filed for divorce. All along, Whitfield's aunt, who owned the land on the Kinchafoonee where the longhouse was, said she they told her it was being used for a hunting lodge. In a way it was. The prey was young girls.

Sometimes waitresses from the Monkey Palace went out to the creek and traded sex for money, but when police raided the longhouse the day I was shot, they found only the two missing teenage girls from Brooks County, Ana Flores and Gabriela Molina. The girls were locked in separate bedrooms and terrified. Unhurt but terrified.

*

The day Abby shot Pearl, she called Mickey from Warren's house and told him what had happened. He said he'd meet us at the hospital.

Mickey said he had something he needed to tell us. At that point I thought nothing would surprise me, but I was wrong.

"I want you two to go back to the newsroom, clean out your desks. You're both fired, goddamnit."

"What?" I said. "Fired for what? Doing our jobs?"

"For doing what I asked you *not* to do," Mickey said. "For risking your lives by going back to that goddamn creek. That's why I'm firing you. Both of you. You're good reporters, but I'm not putting up with any more shit from you two. Got it?"

"Mickey, you don't really mean that, do you?" Abby said. "Fired? After what we've been through."

Thirty seconds passed as Mickey sucked his Marlboro down to his toes. He blew a cloud of smoke that reminded me of what I had seen after Abby shot Pearl.

"No, goddamnit, I'm not going to fire you. I should but I'm not. If I do fire you, I may wait until after you write this story for tomorrow's paper. We'll see how Maynard types with one hand. You two need to get back to work."

"I'll take care of the writing," Abby said. "We'll have something for tomorrow. All of our sources are easy to get to and ready to talk. That won't be a problem."

"Yeah, and you got to write yourself in it," Mickey said.

"We'll work it out," Abby said.

"Good," Mickey said. "And Maynard, I am glad you're not dead. I do want to keep you two around for a while. Little longer anyway. Good job on this, but you two worry the shit out of me."

"I like not being dead, too," I said.

"Well, if I was you, I'd be good to Abby for the rest of your life," Mickey said. "That's a helluva thing she did."

"The rest of my life and longer," I said.

"Do you two need anything from me right now?" Mickey said.

"No, we're headed back to the newsroom," Abby said.

"Good, nowhere else," Mickey said. "Nowhere else."

As Mickey left the emergency room, Detective McGill was walking toward us drinking coffee from a white Styrofoam cup.

"I got something for you," McGill said. "Abby, I want you to have this."

He handed her the silver crucifix that was removed from Maria Rios' body the morning she was found off Palmyra Road.

"This needs to go to her uncle down in Camilla," McGill said. "I want you two to take it to him. You figured all this out before we did. I'm going to make a phone call down there today to try to get word to him about the arrests, but you go down and deliver this to him tomorrow."

Abby took the chain and silver crucifix and held it up and inspected it as if it was a sacred object. And it was to her.

"We'll drive down first thing in the morning," Abby said. "We'll take care of it."

She placed the chain and crucifix that said MARIA and GOD IS LOVE, around her neck as we walked out of the emergency room and drove to the newsroom.

CHAPTER 38

The morning after our story appeared about the arrest and confession of Pearl, and the arrest of others involved in the crimes in the woods along the Kinchafoonee Creek, we returned to Mitchell County to find Maria's uncle.

We wanted to return to Gabriel Rios the crucifix Maria was wearing when she was killed.

Abby wore the crucifix and had slept with it on at my house the night before. I woke before she did and saw that she had her right hand over the cross. She fell asleep that way.Abby drove us to work that morning in her Blue Plymouth Duster, Baby Blue. Because of my injured arm, she had done all the typing on the story that Mickey had played on page one, above the fold. We shared the byline, but she did the writing.

We left the newsroom for Mitchell County around nine that morning. It would be another punishing day with temperatures rising to the upper nineties and the humidity thick enough to slow your breathing. It was good not to be returning to the Kinchafoonee Creek.

We drove south again on U.S. Highway 19 and hoped to find Gabriel Rios in the vegetable fields or in the warehouse on his forklift.

"I just have to ask you one question, Abby. I've been thinking about this since yesterday."

"You're like all the rest of those nosey reporters. All you want to do is ask questions. Well, I've had enough of it. I'm not answering anymore. Not even off the record. And by the way, that's a funny thing to say. *Off the record*. Can't you just leave people alone?"

"No, not you. Ever. I'll never leave you alone."

"What is it? Ask me. Go ahead and ask me."

"When did you know you were going to be able to pull the trigger? To shoot Pearl. Was it when you left me and Hanahan? Or was it when Pearl shot at you? When was it?"

"You tell me," Abby said. "What do you think?"

"What do I think? Hell, I was scared shitless the whole time in the woods and figured you were too. Who wouldn't be? I wasn't the one who shot Pearl. You did that. I never knew that side of you. So tell me when was it? When did you decide you could do it?"

"John, I didn't know that side of me, either. But at that point in the woods, I had long made my mind up."

"What do you mean?"

"I made up my mind the day they found Maria and you wrote the story and told me how awful it was. You told me what the cops told you. What happened to her was evil. But John, she was just like me."

"Just like you? How were you two alike? You never met her. We didn't know much about her life. We knew she had dark hair and dark eyes like you. She was pretty like you. Is that what you mean?"

"No, not at all," Abby said. "That's not what I'm talking about. That's not it."

"What is it then?"

"Dreams, John. We shared the same dreams. A chance to be good and do good in this life. To live a full life and love others. Maria had those dreams, I know she did. That's what I mean."

"So you knew the day Maria's body was found off Palmyra Road that you were now capable of shooting someone? I don't know if that makes sense, Abby."

"In a way, I guess. I guess that's right. I don't care if it makes sense or not."

"I'm a reporter. Be specific."

"You should know the truth by now," Abby said.

"Tell me anyway."

"I knew when we got on this story, I was going to do anything I could to find out who did this to Maria. And to stop it from happening again."

"Now that's a damn good quote."

"Most *good* quotes are true quotes."

I put my left arm around Abby's neck. I eased closer to her and kissed her three times on her right cheek. I stayed close to her for a few moments. The only sounds in the car was from the humming of its air conditioning and her eight-track tape player.

Neil Young was singing and it was from the album *Harvest*. The song was "Heart of Gold:" *I want to live, I want to give/I've been a miner for a heart of gold/It's these expressions I never give that keep me searching for a heart of gold/And I'm getting old...*

We arrived at the vegetable warehouse where Gabriel Rios was operating a yellow forklift and loading boxes of big red tomatoes into a truck. He saw us walking toward him and got off his forklift to greet us.

His blue T-shirt was soaked with sweat. He wore jeans with holes in the knees, worn-out boots, and a straw hat with a green band around it. He spoke before we did.

"I know what happened to my Maria. I know now who did that thing to her. Juan read the paper. His English better than mine. I can only read a few words."

Gabriel shook my left hand, then took his hat off and bowed his head in front of Abby in a display of respect and appreciation. It was a tender moment in a story full of violence and evil.

"Thank you two for what you did. I thank you so much. I know God was watching over you with Maria at His side. I know this to be true."

"Mr. Rios, you're very kind," Abby said. "We are here to give you something."

Abby took the chain and crucifix from her neck and handed it to Gabriel Rios. He held it in his right palm. He was quiet for several seconds and so were we.

"My brother, Maria's father, gave this to her. She said when she wore this, nothing would hurt her. He wanted her to come to America one day. To become a doctor and come back home and help her people. He said there were good people in America. You two are good people."

"We're glad we could return this to you, Mr. Rios," Abby said. "We're so sorry about what happened. We're so sorry. I would've loved to have met Maria."

"No, this is not right," he said. "This is not the way it should be. This is not what God wants."

"What do you mean?" I said.

Gabriel Rios placed Maria's chain and crucifix around Abby's neck. He made the sign of the cross, bowed his head again and then kissed Abby on her forehead.

Abby embraced Gabriel and now I could see tears coming down their cheeks. They held on to each other a few seconds before releasing.

"This is what God wants," Gabriel said. "This is what my lovely Maria wants. This is what she tells me to do. I hear her from heaven. Now you hear her, too."

AUTHOR'S NOTE

Thank you for reading this book. I am fortunate to have the opportunity to tell these stories. *Monkey Palace* is the third installment of the John Maynard and Abby Sinclair series. And there will be others. I'm having too much fun to stop.

Thanks again to Rosemary Barnes of Atlanta who has edited all three books. Her insights have made my manuscripts better. And thanks to my wife, Phyllis, for her constant help and encouragement.

I live and write in the country outside of Fayetteville, Georgia. A beautiful place where the owls, hawks, and coyotes all sing their own songs.

My books are available on Amazon.

www.bill.lightle.com